"We meet again," I s   desk.

"Huh?" He look   blinked, then slowly focused his wonderful eyes on my face. "Oh, yeah, you're—Darleen."

I laughed, ignoring the fact that Mrs. Cole had just called the class to order. "I can never remember names, either. I'm Denise—you know, Mitch's friend."

"Oh, yeah, Mitch." He blinked again, but this time when his eyes focused they became very busy, scanning me from head to toe.

I should say something, I thought. *But what? Or I should at least move to my seat.* I couldn't move, though. I felt frozen to the spot. Paralyzed.

"Unless you're Betsy Ross," Mrs. Cole began, "and are about to demonstrate how you made the first flag, would you kindly take your seat, Miss Dreyer? As for you, Mr. Rogers, we're supposed to be studying American history here, not anatomy."

As the hoots and hollers rang out in the classroom I felt myself turn crimson.

Other books in the FIRST KISS series:

THE PERFECT COUPLE
Helen Santori

BANTAM BOOKS
TORONTO • NEW YORK • LONDON • SYDNEY • AUCKLAND

THE PERFECT COUPLE

A BANTAM BOOK   0 553 40090 8

Originally published in U.S.A. by
Ballantine Books, a division of Random House Inc.

Produced by Butterfield Press, Inc.
133 Fifth Avenue
New York, New York 10003

First publication in Great Britain

PRINTING HISTORY
Bantam Edition published 1990

Bantam Books are published by Transworld Publishers Ltd.,
61–63 Uxbridge Road, Ealing, London W5 5SA,
in Australia by Transworld Publishers (Australia) Pty. Ltd.,
15–23 Helles Avenue, Moorebank, NSW 2170, and in New
Zealand by Transworld Publishers (N.Z.) Ltd., Cnr. Moselle
and Waipareira Avenues, Henderson, Auckland.

Reproduced, printed and bound in Great Britain by
BPCC Hazell Books
Aylesbury, Bucks, England
Member of BPCC Ltd.

Chapter 1

"Did you see that pass? Isn't Ty sensational?" I screamed. I jumped to my feet, pulling my best friend Kim Harris along with me. "There was no way Gordie could miss scoring. Ty practically put the ball in his hands."

"I'll admit it was a good pass, but the game isn't important. That's why they're playing it on a Friday afternoon instead of at night like most of the other games," Kim said. "We always beat Sunnydale." She shook off my hand and sat down.

"So what?" I retorted. "Ty still made a great play." I would have cheered some more, but everyone else had stopped and sat down, so I did, too. By now Kim was studying the new shade of polish on her nails, holding her hand this way and that to view it from all angles.

"What do you think?" she inquired, arching a delicately penciled brow. "Is this color too loud?"

"*Loud*?" I said. "Just because it's fire-engine red? Of course not! It's about as drab as that shocking pink top you're wearing."

If I have something to say I usually blurt it right out, without resorting to sarcasm. But I was hurt and angry that Kim refused to share my excitement over Ty's play. I was always enthusiastic about anything that interested her—from a new hairstyle to a new boyfriend. Well, she could admire her red nail polish all she wanted to. She wasn't going to drag a compliment out of me—even though the bright color did look terrific against her golden hair and china-blue eyes.

I was going to sulk for a while and not say anything, but after a few seconds I couldn't hold back. "You could at least admit that Ty is a great player," I said. "How many sophomores get to be quarterbacks?"

Kim checked the edges of her nails, testing for a rough spot. "I still say we didn't need that touchdown," she said absently. "So why didn't he let up a little bit? Some guys don't like to beat up on a weaker team."

"He plays with all his heart—that's why he didn't let up," I informed her. "But you won't give him credit for anything, will you?" I was almost choking now, but I had enough breath left to get off one last shot. "You've at least got to admit he's the best-looking, most exciting boy in school!"

The instant I'd spoken the last words I clapped a hand over my mouth, but of course it was too late. "I mean," I stumbled on, "that he looks so great on the field—so tall and graceful—and his hair is so dark and shiny where it shows under his helmet. You *had* to notice how his teeth flashed when he smiled and jumped in the air after getting off that pass."

I hadn't meant to blurt out all that, although it was exactly what I was thinking. I'd only made the situation worse. Kim was staring at me, her blue eyes bigger than I'd ever seen them before.

"You're really stuck on him, aren't you?" she gasped. When I started to speak she held up a scarlet-tipped hand. "No, don't bother to deny it, Denise Dreyer, because I'm beginning to add things up. I've noticed how you look at Ty in the halls, and the way you're always dragging his name into the conversation, but I thought it was because you're such a sports fan. But"—she shook her head sorrowfully, as if she'd just learned that I'd contracted a serious, possibly fatal illness—"Ty Rogers!" she lamented. "Why him, Denny? Of all the boys in Bayside High, why him?"

"Why you and Randy?" I countered, although I knew the comparison was ridiculous. She and Randy were both popular, great-looking people, like Ty. But me—I'd never even had a date.

Kim ignored my question. "When did it start, Denny?" She spoke gently as if she were asking when I'd first learned that I wasn't long for this world.

I hated her sympathy, but I'd kept my secret for three whole weeks, and I just had to share it with someone. Kim was my best friend, and when the chips were down I knew I could count on her. I *had* to count on her, it suddenly struck me, because I had a plan to attract Ty's attention and I'd need her help to make it work.

"It started—," I began. Then before I could go on, the first half ended. The Cougars headed for the locker room. Ty whipped off his helmet, and his shining, dark head towered above the other team members as he strode off the field.

Kim nudged me to finish what I'd started to say, but I was too breathless to speak. When Ty disappeared from sight I felt as if my heart had left my body and gone with him. My chest was hollow. I hardly even noticed my good friend Mitch Conley who was trotting off with the substitute players, his rust-red hair glinting in the sun.

Kim thumped me again, putting something into it this time. "Hey, you were going to tell me how long you've had this thing for Ty."

This thing was only the greatest love any woman had ever felt for a man, but it was no use telling Kim that. She thought it was some silly crush like I'd gotten on a rock star once. I drew a tentative breath, and when I found my lungs were working okay again I told her about the day, three weeks ago, when I was standing at the curb in front of the school, waiting to cross the street.

"This red Camaro came roaring up and slammed to a stop right in front of me. I recognized it as belonging to Ty's brother, Hank, and when Ty jumped out, I had the crazy idea he'd stopped for me. All of a sudden I just knew I was in love with him. I've always noticed him—who hasn't—but I'd thought . . . well, I'd never dared to really think about him at all. Then, there he was, just as if he'd come to claim me, and I could admit to myself I'd loved him since eighth grade."

Kim gave the mournful kind of sigh I'd only heard from her before when she'd broken a fingernail, or decided she had nothing in her closet fit to wear.

I heaved a small sigh of my own, then finally went on. "Ty hadn't stopped for me, as it turned out, but for Miriam Sloan, who happened to be standing beside me. He gave her a dazzling smile, took her arm, and then they both got into the backseat of the Camaro. When the car zoomed off he had his arm around her shoulders."

"Oh, Denny." Kim was moaning now as if I were a hurt kitten she'd found beside the road. "Miriam is so popular, and she's so pretty," she observed in a sick-room whisper.

Miriam was *beautiful*, but I ignored Kim's watered-down assessment of her looks. "I've dreamed about Ty every night since," I confided.

"If it were anyone but Ty Rogers." Kim's lovely eyes brimmed with compassion, and I finally decided she'd suffered enough in my behalf, so I told her to cheer up.

"But it was just a few days later that Ty broke up with Miriam. Doesn't that tell you something?"

She was incredulous now. "You mean he did notice you that day? Denny, why didn't you tell me before? Has he said anything—asked you out?"

"No, nothing like that." I waved a hand in the air, indicating that that was an unimportant detail. "He *will* notice me before long, though, and he *will* ask me out."

Kim spoke in a low, apologetic voice. "I think you should know, Denny, that Ty is seeing Gloria Putnam now."

I grinned mysteriously. "Of course he is. He's going with one girl after another because he hasn't found the right one yet."

"*You're* the right girl for him?" She still spoke in that soft, apologetic tone. When I nodded she said, "But what if he never discovers that? What if he never even notices you?"

"He will." I paused, then stated quietly, "You see, I have a plan."

"Tell me!" Kim squealed, forgetting she was fifteen and bouncing up and down like a child.

I didn't answer her right away because the team was coming out for the second half, and with the applause I couldn't have made myself heard without shouting. I held up my index finger to signify that I'd tell her in a minute.

The substitutes came out first, and I waved as Mitch looked up to where he knew I'd be sitting. He waved back, giving me the big grin that put a dimple in his left cheek. As usual, his rust-colored hair tumbled over his forehead, and I could feel the warmth of his blue-green eyes all the way up in the stands.

When he saw that Kim was with me he waved to her, too. The three of us had grown up in the same neighborhood, had been like a brother and two sisters until Kim was ten and began to get interested in clothes and boys. I was a tomboy, so Mitch and I continued to play ball, or to work at some project. Lately we'd been collecting and selling aluminum cans.

Kim was jabbing my arm, wanting me to tell her what my plan was, but now the first-string team was running onto the field and I was breathless again. Ty was swaggering a little bit, but it didn't look show-offy when he did it. How could he help knowing he was good? It wasn't until he went into a huddle with the other players that I turned to Kim.

"My plan is a little complicated," I told her, "I'd better not try to clue you in right now. Can you come home with me after the game?"

"Yes, I guess so. Randy has orchestra. But please, Denny, just give me a hint."

"I honestly can't," I told her. "I didn't get the idea until this morning when Mitch and I both missed the bus and walked to school together. It just popped into my mind. But I haven't worked out all the bugs yet, so I need some more time to think—"

"Mitch?" she cut me off. "What's he got to do with it?"

Only everything, I thought. Aloud I said, "Later. I'll tell you everything later."

She gave me her most enchanting smile. "Can't you at least give me a hint?" she coaxed.

"No," I said firmly. "I don't want you

picking my idea to pieces before I get a chance to perfect it."

She frowned. "I bet you're going to drop your books at Ty's feet to get his attention." I shook my head, and she tried again. "Are you going to throw yourself in the path of his brother's car? I wouldn't put anything past you when you've made up your mind to do something."

I moved my fingers across my lips in a zipping motion, indicating I didn't intend to say another word, so she finally gave up. Not for the world would I have admitted I'd considered the two courses she'd mentioned, and dismissed them both—the first because it was trite, the second because it was too drastic, even for me.

Packed in as we were on the late bus home, Kim couldn't even expect me to discuss anything confidential, so I used the travel time to think over my scheme. I knew that the girl I was now wouldn't attract Ty's attention if she breezed into Bayside wearing only a string bikini. That meant I had to change who I was, and for that I'd need Kim's help. She knew all about makeup and clothes, how to talk to boys, and act around them. If I could only convince her my plan had a chance I knew she'd do what she could to turn me into the kind of girl who'd appeal to Ty.

I considered what she'd have to work

with. My hair was medium brown, and hung straight as a mop to just above my shoulders. My eyes were hazel. There was nothing special about my features, but on the other hand none of them were grossly flawed. I'd grown a couple of inches in the last few months without gaining any additional weight. Kim was bound to appreciate that when it came to picking out some new, eye-catching clothes for me.

We moved to the front as the bus approached our stop, ignoring the horseplay and whistles of the boys we had to brush against in the aisle. The whistles, of course, were directed at Kim, although she always pretended they were for both of us, and I went along rather than argue about it. We got off at Poplar.

The town of Bayside is south of San Francisco in an area known as Silicon Valley because of the electronics industry that has grown up there—computer chips, and all that. Our neighborhood is in the old part of town, while most of the people connected with the electronics companies live in new housing tracts across the highway. None of us mixed with the kids from those families. They were always getting transferred, so what was the use of making friends with them? Besides, they always seemed to act as if they were a cut above the rest of us.

"Is your mother home?" Kim asked as we

walked up the street to the white, two-story Colonial house where I'd lived all my life.

We usually go to my house because Kim's mother is a member of the Little Theatre, a local drama group, and is always rehearsing. It can be pretty unsettling to walk into the kitchen and see her staring at her ketchupy, bloodstained hands while speaking in dramatic tones. Lady Macbeth was her favorite role.

"No," I told Kim. "This is the day Mom puts her column to bed." My mother writes a home-and-garden column for the *Weekly Courier,* and every Friday she takes it downtown for the next week's newspaper.

When we reached my house I led the way to the kitchen. "Cola or root beer?" I asked.

Kim shrugged. "Whatever. Mostly I want to hear how you plan to get Ty Rogers to notice you."

I tossed her a can of cola and grabbed a package of corn chips. "Let's make ourselves comfortable," I said.

That meant going upstairs to my room, kicking off our shoes, and pounding the two big cushions on the floor beside the windows into the right shape for sitting. When we'd done all that and popped the tabs on our sodas, I told Kim what I had in mind.

"I'm going to start dating Mitch," I announced quietly.

"*What*?" Kim gasped. "I didn't dream there was anything between you and Mitch.

I thought you were just pals. But, hey, wait a minute! You said you were in love with Ty. What's this all about, Denny?"

Kim had surprised me dozens of times in the past with news of whom she was dropping, and whom she was starting up with, but it was the first time I'd ever sprung anything like this on her. I savored the reversal of our roles for a minute while I took a leisurely sip of my drink.

"A chip?" I said, extending the bag to her.

"No!" she screamed. "And I'm going to throttle you if you don't tell me what's going on. Who is it you're really in love with—Ty or Mitch?"

Even Hitchcock didn't drag the suspense out too long, so I tossed the chips aside, carefully put down my cola, and for the first time I stated my idea aloud. First I reminded Kim of that fateful day when I'd discovered I was in love with Ty. Then I reminded her of what good friends Mitch and I had always been, and still were.

"I'm sure Ty will notice me if I start to date," I went on. "I've been watching him the last three weeks, and I've noticed he doesn't pay the slightest attention to a girl unless she's with a guy. He'd never look at a girl who hung around with other girls. So tomorrow, when Mitch and I are collecting cans, I'm going to ask him to pretend we're going together."

The way Kim stared at me and sputtered something unintelligible, I was sure she was going to rip my idea to shreds once she found her voice. But then with a little shake of the head she fell silent, and I could see her turning my idea over in her mind, looking at it this way and that, as she'd studied her new nail polish a while ago.

Suddenly I was the one who couldn't stand the suspense. "Well, what do you think?" I leaned forward, holding my breath as if she were an oracle.

Finally the oracle spoke. "Your idea just might fly, at that . . . if Mitch comes through for you. It wouldn't work if he was a wimpy little guy, but he isn't. He's husky— and nice-looking—and he plays on the football team, even though he isn't first string. Ty would notice any girl he went around with. The way I see it, Mitch is the only problem. As good-natured as he is, I can't believe he'll go for such a deal. What boy would want to escort a girl around so she could attract another guy's attention?"

I brushed aside her question with a wave of the hand. "If that's all you're worried about, forget it. Mitch would do anything in the world for me, just like I would for him." I stuck my hand under her nose. "Look! I broke two fingernails the other day helping him change his bicycle tire. I'm always willing to go around looking at cars with him even though he won't be able to drive for almost a year. All he has to do is whistle under my window, and I go running out, ready for anything he's got in mind. So why shouldn't he do something like this for me?"

"Umm," Kim said, her brow puckered in thought.

I could see my idea was beginning to take hold with her. She'd wished for a long time that I'd start dating. When she finally jumped up and began to rummage through my closet I knew she was going to help me.

"Nothing!" she said emphatically after inspecting my wardrobe—if it could be called that. "We'll have to do some shopping this weekend. There's your hair, too. Thank goodness you don't have it chopped off at your ears anymore. It's a nice length for one of those soft-body perms."

For about five minutes she stood over me, hands on her hips, studying me as if I were something on a glass slide. Her frown grew so deep I thought she'd decided I was hopeless. In the end, though, she gave a little nod and asked how early I could get away the next day.

I reminded her that I'd planned to go with Mitch in the morning to collect aluminum cans. "And I can't go back on my word. We never do that to each other. Oh, if only I hadn't said I'd go," I groaned. "We could be at the mall when it opens."

"Don't worry about it," Kim said. "That'll

give you a good chance to talk to him, and find out if he'll go along with your scheme."

"He'll go along with it," I assured her.

She looked skeptical and I could understand her doubts. She didn't realize the kind of friendship Mitch and I had. She'd had lots of boyfriends, but she'd never really been *friends* with a boy since she was a little kid and hardly knew the difference between boys and girls.

"Just be sure you're home by noon," she said. "As soon as you've showered and changed, we'll take off. Oh, and make sure you bring along a fistful of credit cards."

"Sure thing," I told her. Just then we heard Mom's car pull into the driveway.

"I'd better go," Kim said, heading downstairs. We reached the front door just in time to open it for my mother.

"Oh, hello, girls," Mom said. "What mischief have you two been cooking up?" That had been her standard greeting for us ever since Kim and I had been alone in the house when we were six, and had tried to make cookies. We'd lost control of the mixer, and I don't think Mom was convinced yet that she'd gotten all the dough off the walls and ceiling.

Kim and I giggled, mostly to please Mom. When my mother had gone upstairs Kim said we'd have to remember to buy some nail-mend the next day. "Fixing Mitch's bicycle tire has not done your nails any

good, Denny," she said, glaring distastefully
at my hands. "You can't go around with
broken nails if you want to attract a boy like
Ty."

"What's nail-mend?" I asked. Being a tomboy hadn't prepared me very well for being a
femme fatale.

"You'll find out tomorrow," Kim told me.

As I closed the door behind her I had the
feeling that the next day I was going to be
initiated into some mysterious female cult,
and that I'd never be quite the same again.

That night at the dinner table I sprang it on
Mom that I had to do some heavy shopping.
"How's my credit?" I asked.

"A-one," she told me. "You didn't spend
nearly as much as I thought you would at
the beginning of the term. Remember, I told
you that as a sophomore you'd need something dressier than jeans and T-shirts, but
you said it didn't matter. What's up—a
party?"

"Not exactly," I said, "although I probably
will be going to parties and dances before
long."

Dad looked up from the casserole we
always have the day Mom spends at the
Courier. "Of course you will, Denny," he
said. "You'll be the belle of the ball, too."

Everyone should have such a fan.

I was glad when my parents began to talk

about my older sister, Bonnie, who was a freshman at a San Francisco college. They were looking forward to her coming home for Thanksgiving.

"I just hope she isn't getting run down from all the dating, and that heavy schedule she's carrying," Mom fussed.

Suddenly it occurred to me that Bonnie hadn't started to date until she was almost sixteen. She wasn't a tomboy, but she read a lot and was satisfied to go around with other girls until she'd gotten interested in Frankie Lasko. It didn't last long with Frankie, but after going with him for a while she had plenty of other dates. That's the way it worked. You just had to break in. I smiled as I picked at the salmon casserole, thinking that the second Dreyer girl was about to make her mark at Bayside. Except there was just one boy I cared to date—Ty Rogers.

Mom and Dad almost always went to a movie on Friday night. I usually went with them, although I felt funny sometimes if someone from school saw me at the movie theater with my parents. Tonight I definitely didn't want to take that chance. "You run along," I told Mom. "I'll take care of the kitchen."

"Are you sure, dear?" She gave me a long look, and I knew she could see I was growing up. I couldn't be sure if she was happy about it or not. Her lips were smiling, but there was sort of a misty look in her eyes.

"I'm sure," I said.

While I stacked the dishwasher and cleaned the stove and sink, I went over my plan, and for the first time some nasty little doubts crept into my mind. What if Mitch, for some reason, let me down? Or what if he went along with my scheme, but Ty still didn't notice me? What if I were doomed to live the rest of my life without Ty's dreamy, dark eyes ever gazing into mine? What if I never got to speak to him, or—my heart fluttered in my chest—feel his kiss?

I cut a picture of Ty from the school paper after the last football game. Game Hero was the caption under it.

When I went up to my room I unlocked my diary and took out the picture. Carefully smoothing it out, I looked at it for a long time, adoring each perfect feature of Ty's face.

"Good night, sweet prince," I whispered at last, and then I gently folded the picture and placed it back between the pages of my diary.

Suddenly I thought of Mitch, who was all-important to my plan. I went to the window, and though I couldn't see his house which was on the next block, I smiled in that direction. I wondered if he could sense that tomorrow our friendship would undergo a drastic change.

Chapter 2

Saturday we had a monstrous breakfast, as usual. Over her second cup of coffee, Mom—as usual—asked me what my plans were for the day.

"Mitch and I are going to collect cans till noon, then Kim and I are going to the mall."

Daddy beamed at me. "That Mitch is a fine boy," he said.

"A very fine boy," Mom agreed.

Oh, no! They'd talked it over and decided Mitch was the boy I'd had in mind when I said I'd soon be going to parties and dances. Not that I could blame them. He was practically the only boy I knew. Still, it seemed to me *they* should know better. How romantic did they think it would be for Mitch and me to date, after practically growing up in the same nest? As a little kid he'd spent almost

as much time at my house as his own, and
vice versa.

But if Mitch agreed to my plan, I would be
dating him at first, so I decided to let it go. "I
suppose you and Dad are going to play golf
and have lunch at the club," I said.

"If your father has the courage to take me
on again after last Saturday," Mom replied.
She teased Dad with her eyes, which were a
darker hazel than mine. It was comforting
to see them still flirting after so many years
together.

After breakfast, we all chipped in to
clear the breakfast dishes and straighten
the kitchen. As soon as we'd finished, I
bounded up to my room and got into my
oldest jeans and sneakers and a gray sweat
shirt I hadn't worn for ages because I was
supposed to have put it in the ragbag. If
Mom was going off to the golf course with
Dad, though, maybe I could get away with
wearing it one more time.

As soon as I pulled it over my head, I
saw—or rather felt—that it didn't fit right
anymore. I pulled and tugged, but it was too
tight across the chest. When I looked in the
mirror on the closet door I saw that I'd done
some more developing. It had started some
time ago, but just lately, as if there was
something magic about turning fifteen, I'd
really become curvy.

I felt kind of excited, although when I'd
stripped off the sweat shirt and tossed it in

the cast-off bag Mom hopefully kept in my closet, it was a little bit like ditching an old friend.

I put on one of the loose cotton shirts I'd inherited from Bonnie when she'd gone away to college, then I finger-combed my hair and ran down to the garage. Two minutes later I braked my bike in front of Mitch's ranch-style house. He was already on his ten-speed and scowling, which he didn't do often.

"Where have you been?" he growled. "You're ten minutes late. You don't think we'll be the only ones out looking for cans today, do you? You know the easy ones get snatched up first."

What was I supposed to do—tell him I'd had to change shirts at the last minute because of certain changes that had taken place in my body?

"If you're in such a hurry, let's go," I said. Then I thought I'd better not snap at him no matter how grouchy he acted. I had a pretty big favor to ask of him, although I hadn't thought it was so big until Kim pointed out that it was something most boys wouldn't do.

Before we could pedal off, Mitch's twelve-year-old sister Susie came out on the front porch. She'd probably be cute in a couple of years—might even act like a civilized person—but right now she was a knobby-kneed brat with a mouthful of hardware and the manners of a wolverine.

"When are you going to be back?" she yelled at Mitch, hands on her skinny hips.

"Oh, some time before dark, I imagine," Mitch teased her as he sometimes teased me.

"You'd better not be so smart!" Susie warned. "I don't care if you ever come back, but Mama wants to know."

"Tell her I'll be back by noon. And any time you want to go to charm school, I'll spring for the tuition. Maybe they'll teach you to say hello to people." Mitch tried to scowl at her, but he didn't do a very convincing job of it.

Still, the brat suddenly turned angel. "Hi, Denny," she chirped, her braces glittering in the sun.

"Hi, Susie!"

As Mitch and I started off, I remarked, "Nice kid." The way he'd teased Sue, I knew he was already back in his usual good mood, so everything was going to be okay.

"Sometimes she is," he agreed with a big-brother grin.

At the corner I asked what he thought of trying Lookout Point. "We haven't been there for a while, and we might get lucky. Kim and I are going to the mall this afternoon, and I'd kind of like to get home early."

"Sure. Let's try the Point."

Last summer we'd both had jobs with the recreation department, helping to clean up trash from the parks and playgrounds. We had to keep the aluminum cans separate from the other trash because they could be sold and recycled. When school started, and our jobs ended, Mitch got the idea of us going into business for ourselves. Plenty of cans were discarded along the streets and roads. Every Saturday we'd been going out and filling a couple of bags. We stored them in Mitch's garage, and when we had enough to make it worthwhile, his dad drove us to the salvage yard where they weighed them and paid us. Mitch was saving his money for a car. I spent mine mostly for sports equipment, like soccer boots and shin guards and my own ball so I could practice at home.

As we started up the hill we had to slow down—all right *I* had to slow down—so I took time to steal a glance at his profile. I remembered what Kim had said about him being nice-looking. I'd never thought much about his looks before. He was just my good old buddy. But now I wondered how another girl would see him.

She'd probably be impressed, I thought. He was really quite handsome with his strong, blunt features, his wild thatch of reddish-brown hair and blue-green eyes that twinkled like sparklers when he smiled . . . which was a lot of the time.

"Want to rest a while?" Mitch stopped and looked back over his shoulder. The grade was really steep now. I was pedaling hard, but still I'd fallen behind.

"I'm okay," I said, trying not to pant. "We don't want anyone to beat us to the Point."

There were usually a lot of cans right out in the open at Lookout Point. People would park there to look out over the canyon, maybe have a soda, and some of them would just toss their empties out the window. I used to think litterbugs should be put in the stocks in front of the county courthouse. Well, I still did, in a way, but if they were going to litter, I couldn't help being glad that some of them at least left the cans out on the paved area, where we didn't have to get poison oak to retrieve them.

When we reached the Point we leaned our bikes against the bank across the road and got busy. I was out of breath, and my legs were trembling, but it had been worth the climb because there were cans everyplace.

There was another reason I was glad we'd come here today. When we filled our bags we'd sit on the bank and look down into the valley while we drank the sodas we'd brought. That would be the perfect time for me to tell Mitch my idea.

"Yuck," I said after a while.

"What's the matter?"

"Somebody stuck a cigarette butt in this can." I had on gloves, but still I hated to pick up cans that were messy.

"Here, I'll get it." Mitch picked up the dirty can and put it in his bag, then tossed a clean one into mine. "That'll make it even."

"Thanks. You're a pal," I said.

"Haven't I always been your pal?" He gave me kind of a shy grin.

Had he always been shy, or was he changing? He wasn't always so protective, either. Once he'd put a worm in my lunch pail and pretended it had crawled out of my apple. I didn't believe him, but still I wouldn't eat an apple for a long time, and he'd roar with laughter when he'd offered me one and I'd refuse it. That seemed like such a long time ago. . . .

When we decided we had had enough for the day we dragged our bags of cans across the road, then sat down on the bank in the shade of a tall eucalyptus tree. I popped the tab on an orange soda, and Mitch opened a cola. When we'd both taken a long, thirsty pull, I finally spoke up.

"We're really good friends, aren't we, Mitch?"

As he turned to look at me, he pushed a tumble of rust-red hair back from his forehead. "The Two Musketeers," he said. When he'd first called us that, I'd reminded him that there were three musketeers, but he'd said that two friends were better than three. "What's on your mind, Dreyer?" he asked.

This was a lot harder than I'd thought it would be, and for a minute I wanted to tell him there was nothing on my mind, I was just making conversation. But he knew me too well for that. I could fool my parents some of the time, but I couldn't fool Mitch any of the time. He *knew* I had something to say, and he wouldn't let me off the hook until I told him what it was.

I gulped air the way I'd just gulped my soda, and then I got it out. "Starting on Monday I want you to pretend to be my boyfriend."

He chuckled. "What do you want us to do—put on a play in the garage? Don't you think we're a little too old for that?"

I'd never felt self-conscious with Mitch before, but now it was all I could do to look into his eyes. My voice was wobbly as I said, "It's nothing like that. But I do need your help, Mitch."

His smile was reassuring. "Just tell me what I can do for you. We're the Two Musketeers—right?"

"What I want us to be is Romeo and Juliet!" I burst out, grateful for the cue he'd thrown me. "And I don't mean for a play. I want us to start going together like a couple. You know—as if we were dating, and sort of in love."

Mitch gaped at me, his mouth almost as wide open as his eyes. "But—why?" he croaked.

I swallowed. This was getting harder by the minute, but somehow I managed to say, "Because I'm in love with Ty Rogers, and he won't notice me if I keep going around with other girls. All you have to do—"

That was as far as I got before Mitch bounded to his feet, his eyes shooting green sparks. "Are you out of your mind?" he yelped. "You want me to go out with you because you're in love with Ty Rogers? What kind of sense does that make?" Before I could try to explain he spat out, "Ty Rogers!" as if it had just gotten through to him who I was talking about. "I didn't think you even knew that guy was alive."

I jumped up, too. "It's the other way around!" I flung back at him. "Ty doesn't know *I'm* alive." I knew I had no right to be angry with Mitch, but I was so disappointed that he was letting me down, I had to get mad or cry—and I hadn't cried since I was a kid, except at the movies, which didn't count. I'd been so sure my old friend would laugh at my scheme and say, sure, he'd help me out.

"That's good," Mitch growled, although he'd simmered down a little bit. "Quite a few girls at Bayside would be better off if that guy *hadn't* noticed they were alive." He paused, then said, "Ty Rogers!" for the third time. Each time he said the name he sounded more disgusted. "I don't know what you see in that showboat." He shook his head as if he were giving up on me.

Whether I had a right to be or not I was suddenly furious with him. "I see that he's the most gorgeous, most exciting boy in school, and I'm going to attract his attention if I have to throw myself in front of his brother's car!" I yelled. I straightened up my bike, put my bag of cans in the rack, and started to climb aboard. My eyes were blurred with tears, and I hardly knew what I was doing. To me a friend was a friend and you helped him out no matter how you felt about what he wanted to do. Mitch had better not whistle under my window again, I thought darkly, and expect me to come dashing out of the house, ready for any dumb thing he wanted me to do. I'd never forget when we went panning for gold in Deer Creek. He'd read someplace that there was still plenty of gold in California. I didn't think there was any in Deer Creek, and I was right. Just the same I'd panned right along with him, and almost got pneumonia from standing in the cold water.

"Hey, where are you going, Denny?" he hollered after me, as I started to push off down the hill. In a few strides he'd caught up with me. "You didn't mean that about throwing yourself under Hank Rogers's car, did you?" He bent over, anxiously studying my face.

I'd never been able to stay mad at Mitch for more than a few minutes. "No, of course not," I said. "I guess I was just doing what Daddy calls my Bette Davis act." I smiled, but then without warning my eyes filled with tears again, and before I could blink them back two big fat ones broke away and ran down my cheeks.

"You're crying!" Mitch gasped.

"I am not!" I couldn't help sniffling, though. It wasn't like me to be weepy and emotional, but I supposed that came from being in love. And Mitch wasn't going to help me, so Ty would never notice me. Never. My life was over almost before it had begun.

"You are, too," Mitch insisted gently. For a minute he looked helpless and bewildered. Then all at once he thrust out his jaw. "We're going to sit down and talk this over." He pulled me off the bike, and wheeled it back where it had been. Dragging my feet—I still didn't think he was going to help me—I followed. When we'd sat down on the bank again he said, "Exactly what do you want me to do, Denny? You know I'll help you if I can. You just caught me by surprise when you said—well, you know."

I was so choked up that Mitch wasn't letting me down, after all, that I couldn't speak right away. For a few seconds I didn't even think about Ty in my relief that Mitch really was the good friend I'd always considered him. Then I remembered what this was all about, and I repeated what I'd said about wanting to attract Ty's attention.

"But he'll never look at me unless I'm going with another boy."

Mitch gave a puzzled frown. "Why would he be interested in you because you're going with another guy? I'd feel the opposite

way—that a girl was off limits if she was
going with someone else."

I could see where Mitch would feel that
way, but Ty was more competitive . . .
which might be the reason he was a great
athlete while Mitch was only second string.

"That just happens to be the way Ty is," I
said. "I've been watching him for three
weeks now, and he simply doesn't glance at
a girl who's alone, or with other girls."

Mitch made a grunting sound that wasn't
really a word, then he said, "So you want us
to pretend we're . . . in love."

"Sort of," I replied. "We'll hang out together around school, have sodas at The
Last Straw together, and maybe go to the
movies. We'll laugh and talk and hold
hands, the way a couple does when they're
going together."

Mitch wrinkled his brow, what I could see
of it under his shaggy bangs. Then, looking
away from me, he picked up a handful of
dirt and let it run through his fingers while
he mulled the whole thing over. You could
never hurry Mitch. He didn't rush into
things, but once he'd made up his mind to
do something you could count on him to see
it through to the end.

I waited patiently while the leafy dirt ran
through his fingers. In the meantime, I did
some thinking, too. The way he'd mentioned Ty being a show-off, it struck me that
I might have hit a nerve in asking him to

help me attract his attention. Ty was the star of the football team while Mitch was only a substitute. I could see where Mitch might hate the idea of being a substitute boyfriend, too.

After what seemed like hours, Mitch looked at me, and when he spoke I learned that something entirely different was bothering him.

"There's just one problem I see in all this," he said. "What if I should get interested in another girl? I couldn't very well ask her out if she thought I was serious about you."

"Another girl?" I gasped. For some reason I was stunned at the idea.

"Yeah. I didn't tell you, but a while ago I thought I was in love with Patty McDougal. I'm over it now, but I notice girls a lot these days, and it could happen again at any time."

I knew I shouldn't be surprised that Mitch was beginning to think seriously about girls. He'd been fifteen for quite a while now. It was just that he was always hustling for money so he could buy a car the day he turned sixteen, and he was so busy keeping his grades up so he could get into Stanford, where his dad had gone, that I guess I didn't think he'd have time to fall in love.

"Patty McDougal?!" I said as it suddenly got through to me who he'd been talking about. She had massive freckles all over her, and she still hadn't lost all her baby fat. I didn't want to put her down to Mitch, though, so I caught myself in time. "She's— real pretty," I said.

"Yeah, I guess," Mitch said, "but she giggles too much. I began to notice it after a while, and it got on my nerves."

"Do I giggle too much?" I asked, suddenly anxious.

"You don't giggle, exactly," he said. "When you laugh it sounds kind of like my mother's music box. Tinkling, you know."

I was so relieved, I did giggle, and then we both burst out laughing. Finally I remembered how serious this was, and I told Mitch that if he got interested in another girl we'd just pretend to break up. "The same way we will if—when—Ty gets interested in me."

Mitch wrapped his arms around his knees and looked off across the road where the first car of the day had just pulled in. He wasn't looking at the car, though. All I could see was his snub-nosed profile, but I knew he was brooding about what I wanted him to do.

Finally he straightened up and looked at me. "I don't know about that guy, Denny. I'd hate to see you hurt, and the way he goes from one girl to another—"

"That's because he hasn't met the right girl yet," I interrupted.

"And you think you're the right girl for him?"

He'd practically echoed Kim's words when

I'd told her the same thing, and I began to worry about something besides getting Mitch's help.

"Don't you think I'm pretty enough for him to like me?" Mitch was a boy, too. Maybe he knew I had no chance with Ty, or any other attractive boy.

He held out his hands in a helpless gesture. "Gosh, I have no idea of how you look to other guys, Denny. That would be like me trying to guess how Sue looks to those little twerps in her seventh-grade class. You're just Denny to me."

"Yeah, I know," I mumbled. "The same way you're just Mitch to me."

We were both silent for a while, then Mitch said, "I've got a couple of candy bars. Let's eat them to seal our bargain."

"Then we have a bargain? You're going to help me out?"

"Sure. We go into action Monday morning. That's· what you want, isn't it?"

"Oh, Mitch!" I threw my arms around his neck, as a big bubble of excitement burst inside me. "You're the best friend a girl ever had!"

"Hey, you're choking me!" Laughing, he pulled my arms from around his neck. "So we're buddies," he said with a shrug. "If I were in love you'd do the same for me, wouldn't you?"

For some reason I hesitated a second before declaring, "Of course I would."

He gave sort of a wry smile as if he thought it was funny for us to want to help each other attract someone else's attention. His voice was a little bit gravelly when he asked if I wanted to eat the candy bar now or on the way home.

"On the way home," I told him. "If I know Kim, she's probably running a fever by now she's so anxious for us to get to the mall. She's going to help me pick out some cute clothes to further the cause."

Mitch looked shocked. "Kim is in on your scheme?"

"Yes, but she's the only one who is," I assured him. "And you know Kim. She'd never give away a secret."

"Umm," he agreed. "But I don't want anybody else to know. I feel stupid enough about the whole thing without everybody in the world knowing about it." He gave me my candy bar. Just as we got on our bikes the young couple in the sports car across the road threw two soda cans out the window. Mitch and I exchanged glances. "We'll get them next time, he said.

We laughed as we started down the hill. It was good to be laughing with my old buddy again.

Chapter 3

As soon as I'd showered and gotten into jeans and a T-shirt, Kim and I left for the mall. She was thrilled that Mitch was going to help me, and eager to do her share. As we started the long walk, she flashed a shopping list a yard long.

"These are things we just *have* to get."

When we got back to my house three hours later I felt as if we'd been gone for three days. I'd never known there were little hideaway boutiques that sold nothing but underwear or makeup or miniskirts. There were, though, and Kim dragged me from one to another till I was on the point of collapse. It was only when I told her I didn't dare charge another item that she decided we could get by with what we'd already bought.

Back in my own room, I dropped my

packages on the floor and flopped on the bed. "I'm beat," I groaned. "I wouldn't be this tired if I'd run a marathon."

"Well, you've just been on a shopping marathon," Kim said very seriously. "But it's only your first one. You'll get used to it. Now, sit at the dressing table. I'm going to give you your perm."

"You are not! People in intensive care don't get perms."

"All right," she relented. "We'll do the perm tomorrow—and the makeup, too. All you have to do now is watch me while I show you how to walk and talk and laugh when you're with a boy. Cute clothes and makeup won't mean a thing if you and Mitch go on acting like friends instead of a couple."

What she said made sense, so I hauled myself to a sitting position, and with two big pillows at my aching back I concentrated on her every move. I'd never dreamed that there was so much to walking. I'd thought you just put one foot after the other until you got where you wanted to go. I'd also thought I knew how to breathe, and to talk and laugh, and to look up at someone who was taller than me.

Not so. It seemed I knew nothing at all about those everyday things, and Kim was still instructing me when my folks got home.

"I guess we'd better knock it off for now," Kim said, "but we'll really get to work tomorrow morning. You don't have to go anywhere, do you?"

"Mom and Dad are going down to San Jose to see Aunt June, but I'll get out of it. I *do* have a lot of homework to do."

We laughed, then she glanced fondly at my closet and the dressing table where all the makeup we'd bought was laid out, along with the perm box.

"Oh, Denny, I'm just dying to see the new you!" she cried.

"So am I." Suddenly bursting with self-confidence, I declared, "You know what, Kim? I'm going to go to the Christmas Ball with Ty. You just wait and see!" The Christmas Ball was the big winter event at Bayside High—they even chose a special couple to be the sweethearts of the dance. I didn't care who the couple turned out to be, but all at once I was determined that Ty was going to be my date.

Kim gave me a doubtful look. "Making up your mind that Ty is going to take you to the Christmas Ball isn't exactly like deciding you're going to make the soccer team," she observed.

That had been my big ambition when school started. I'd made the team with ease, and I refused to admit that this was any different.

"Making up your mind that a boy is going to take you to a dance is *exactly* like deciding you're going to make a team," I insisted. "All you need is determination and know-how. You've given me the know-how, and I already have plenty of determination. Ty is going to take me to the Christmas Ball. You can bet on it!"

For once I was too excited to eat a big Sunday breakfast. After one waffle and two sausages, I shook my head to seconds.

"If I didn't know better I'd say you were in love." Dad had a teasing twinkle in his eyes. "The appetite is always the first thing to go. In the present instance, though, I'd say that you probably ate too much at the mall yesterday."

He didn't seem to realize I was getting too old to be teased. "I didn't go to the mall to eat," I said loftily. "I went there to shop, and except for one skimpy little slice of pepperoni pizza and a chocolate shake that's what I did."

"Did you find some nice things, dear?" Mom asked. "I didn't get a chance to see all your new clothes yesterday."

Before I could answer, the telephone rang. Bonnie always called on Sunday morning, so Mom went to take it. She talked to Bonnie for a while, then Dad went to have a chat with her. Finally it was my turn to go to the phone.

"Hi, Bonnie," I said.

"Hello, Denise."

Usually she called me Denny. Her tone

was different from what it usually was, too, and I began to worry. Was something wrong up there in San Francisco? Was she flunking some of her courses? Or was she just getting run down the way Mom feared?

When she spoke I found out it was none of the above. She acted as if I'd undergone some sort of maturity ritual and all of a sudden I'd become an adult. It was kind of nice, I have to admit.

"Mom told me that you're starting to date," she said. "I'm real happy for you. Mitch is a sweet guy."

I wished I could tell her the truth, that it wasn't Mitch I was interested in, but of course I couldn't. I'd given my word to Mitch that I wouldn't tell anyone but Kim about our little charade, and besides, it wouldn't be right to tell Bonnie what was going on and not tell Mom and Dad.

"Thanks," I mumbled.

"We'll talk it all over when I come home for Thanksgiving," Bonnie said.

"Yeah, that'll be great." Mitch would probably be out of the picture by then, and Ty and I would be going together.

Later Mom and Dad got ready to leave for San Jose. "Sure you don't want to come, dear?" Mom asked. "Your Aunt June would love to see you."

"I'm sure." I'd been sure the last three times she'd asked me. "Kim's coming over. Besides, I have a lot of homework to do."

As soon as the car drove off, Kim dashed across the street. I wasn't sure, because I hadn't had a stopwatch on her, but she'd probably broken an Olympic record. Up in my room she tore open the carton that held the perm, and soon my dressing table was spread with rollers, some little squares of paper, and bottles of various solutions.

"I hope it doesn't come out too frizzy," I said, beginning to get a little bit edgy about the whole thing.

"Do you want a permanent or not?" Kim was in charge, and she wasn't about to let me forget it. I had to give her credit, though, she always deferred to me when it came to sports or math.

"Yes, but—"

"Then sit down and let me get on with it. Here, you can hand me those papers, one at a time."

I was afraid to hope for too much, but when I'd been curled and neutralized, blow-dried and brushed out, my hair swung softly around my shoulders. Somehow it had picked up shadings and highlights so that it was no longer plain brown, but as multicolored as autumn leaves. I was so thrilled I danced around the room.

"This is great, Kim! I never thought I could look like this. You're a genius!"

She gave me a more or less modest smile, then she told me to sit down again. "We'll do your face now."

I wasn't worried about that because makeup could be washed off. Then Kim said she wasn't sure whether we should go with brown eyes or green.

"But my eyes are already hazel," I said in confusion.

"I know, but with eye pencil and shadow, we can bring out different colors in your eyes," Kim informed me. "I'm glad we bought this palette of shadows. We'll experiment until we find out what does the most for you."

In the end my eyes were still hazel, but they looked more green than brown. Kim used blusher to give me cheekbones, and lip gloss to give me what she called a "wide, generous mouth." When she was through, I studied my reflection in the mirror for a long while, then I jumped up and whirled around the room, throwing out my arms . . . wanting to hug the whole world.

"It's going to work!" I announced to the walls and ceiling, and the bed and the dresser. I glanced in the mirror again. I still couldn't believe it was me. "Ty will wonder where I've been all this time."

"Don't get too excited yet," Kim warned. "We still have to work on your personality, but you've given me an idea, dancing around like that. Being vivacious suits you. You'll be all movement and smiles and flirty looks. And teeth. You have good teeth, so you'll laugh a lot, showing off as many of them as you can."

Being made over physically was one thing, but having your whole personality altered was something else. Yet I knew what was behind this and didn't force Kim to spell it out. I wasn't a natural beauty like she was—or the girls Ty went with. My looks alone, even with a lot of goop on my face, wouldn't attract him. My best bet was to develop a lively manner.

"Like this?" I said, throwing back my head and sending forth peals of laughter.

"Well, something like that," Kim said. "We'll work on it later, but now we'd better practice some conversation. When Ty finally notices you, you're not going to talk football or soccer with him. . . . Okay, I'll pretend to be him." In a gruff, would-be male voice she said, "What do you like to do for fun, Denise?"

I tossed my head the way she'd taught me. "Oh, the usual thing—listen to rock, and go to the movies. And *dance*. I'm already looking forward to the Christmas Ball."

"Not bad," Kim said. "Just don't be pushy about the dance. That turns guys off. Why don't you polish your act on Mitch starting tomorrow? Then you'll be ready for Ty."

"Good thinking," I replied. "Now, how about some pizza?"

We went down to the kitchen and I heated up a frozen pizza in the microwave. October is one of the nicest months in the San Francisco Bay area so we took our lunch out on the patio and soaked up some rays while we ate and talked.

"What's Randy doing this weekend?" I asked.

"He's sitting in on a gig with his dad," she told me. "The Eight Steps in San Francisco. They call it that because it's eight steps below street level."

Kim had been going with Randy Dawson since shortly after school started. He lived in another neighborhood, and she hadn't known him till she joined the music club at the beginning of the term. She'd joined mostly because she wanted to belong to a club, not because she was so interested in music. If there'd been a fashion club she would have been the president of it. Once she'd met Randy though, she really did begin to enjoy music.

Pretty soon all she was talking about was Randy Dawson. "He plays the trumpet. His father is a jazz musician—a pro. Isn't that exciting?"

"Your father's a doctor. He saves lives," I'd reminded her.

"Oh, sure, but—" She waved a hand, and I noticed she was wearing a purplish-black nail polish. "You know something else about Randy? He's not interested in how I look, Denny! I don't think he even knows

I'm a blonde. He likes to talk to me—not *at* me, but *to* me!"

I'd thought that Randy, the music maker, would soon go the way of Jerry, the jock, and Brian, the brain. But it turned out that Randy really was different. He was a slender, nice-looking guy with mild brown eyes behind big, owlish glasses. His light brown hair was long and straggly, and he didn't seem to care—or even know—what he was wearing. He treated Kim like she was a real person and not a doll made for boys to admire.

I could see where that appealed to her. She was smart and ambitious and already interested in some kind of fashion career. I was beginning to think Randy might last the whole fall term—maybe the whole year, even.

Kim sighed now. "Sometimes I can't help being jealous of Randy's music. The way he half-closes his eyes when he plays his trumpet, you just know he's in another world."

"I'll probably be jealous of Ty's football," I responded.

It was so much fun to talk, now that I was in love, too, that we could hardly break off to do our homework. Finally we had to, though. She went home, and I went up to my room where I chewed on a pencil for about five minutes before I could even remember what the assignments were.

* * *

By the time Mom and Dad got home I had the potatoes peeled, the carrots scraped, and the roast ready for the oven. Mom came into the kitchen first, through the garage door. Dad always cleaned the car after a trip.

"Denise!" Mom said. She usually called me that only when she was mad at me. I looked at her, wondering what I'd done wrong. Didn't she like my new look? Then I saw that a smile was spreading over her face.

"Your hair looks lovely, dear. And you've put on a little makeup." She walked around me, touching my hair and making little noises as the ends curled around her fingers. Then finally her smile turned sort of misty, the way it did when something reminded her that I was growing up. "My tomboy seems to have turned into a young lady," she murmured.

I'd toned down the makeup some, or she might not have been so pleased. I'd figured out that she was willing to let me grow up, but only a little bit at a time.

Later Dad drank a toast to my new look with his coffee. "To the belle of the ball!"

Of course I thought of the Christmas Ball. And my heart almost leaped out of my chest knowing that—well, hoping anyway, that Ty would be my escort.

Chapter 4

Monday morning Mitch called me. That was unusual on a school morning, but it seemed that nothing was usual anymore.

"We'd better walk to school," he said. "That way more people will see us than if we bike or take the bus. You know how it is the last few blocks. Kids converge from all over. Most of the time Ty rides with his brother, but for all we know, they may drive by and he'll see us together. That'll be a beginning."

Mitch was sure getting into the spirit of the thing. And what he said was true. Still, I groaned at the thought of walking to school. I wasn't wearing my sneakers, but a pair of blue patents with little curved heels. They were comfortable for just walking around, but I wasn't sure how they'd be on a two-mile hike. Well, I supposed that aching arches were a small price to pay if we did no more than get the word out today: Denise Dreyer and Mitch Conley were a twosome.

"See you out front," I said.

Mitch's eyes got so big when I ran out the gate that he looked as if he was wearing goggles. "Is that really you?"

My hair, lively from the brushing I'd given it, bounced around my shoulders. I hadn't put on too much makeup, but I had given myself features where before I'd just had a face. From the mix-and-match things I'd bought Saturday I'd chosen to put on a gray miniskirt, a white blouse, and a vest the same rich blue as my shoes.

"Did I look so awful before?" I asked, practicing my flirting with a mock frown.

"I didn't notice how you looked before," Mitch said.

"Oh." I swallowed, then said, "You look nice, too."

He had on his acid-washed jeans and a green polo shirt that went terrifically with his blue-green eyes and reddish hair which he'd slicked back with some kind of gel. So far only one small strand had broken away to fall across his brow. I thought of pushing it back, then decided not to, although it would be good practice for me. Ty's hair sometimes fell over his forehead, too. Yet when it did it had sort of an arranged look, so maybe he wouldn't appreciate me pushing it back.

"Where's Kim?" Mitch asked.

"She called and said she was running late, so told us to go on. I think maybe she had the idea it would be better if we started out alone. She sure is a terrific friend. You, too." I shot him a smile as we started down the street.

He didn't answer. For a minute he looked kind of angry about something, but then he lightened up. "You think we should hold hands? There are some kids on the next block."

"I . . . don't know," I said. I had a strange feeling it might change things between us if we held hands. I remembered what Mitch had said about responding to girls these days. I *was* a girl, even though we were just friends. And now I looked like a girl with my new clothes and makeup and permanent.

"We want to make this look good," he urged, "in case Ty drives by. The sooner he gets interested in you, the sooner we can go back to being pals, instead of Romeo and Juliet."

For a second I felt a tiny bit hurt. He didn't have to hate being Romeo to my Juliet all that much, did he? Still, I slipped my hand into his. I was surprised at how big his hand felt around mine. His skin was warm and soft, except for the calluses on his palms. I had some calluses, too. I wondered if he'd noticed. Then I thought of something a lot more important. I'd better not hold hands with Ty for a while. Calluses would turn him off even faster than broken fingernails.

The kids we caught up with had all been part of our crowd since grade-school days. They all picked up on my changed appearance. Debbie Conklin told me I looked nice, but Jean Sorenson tried to cut me down.

"Who are you supposed to be—Miss Bayside High of October?" Her smile was more like a sneer.

Remembering that only a short time ago she'd asked me when I was going to grow up and get interested in something besides sports, I didn't bother to answer her. She'd never been one of my favorite people.

A minute later Carol Hodges came running out of her yard. She was my second-best friend, although we hadn't seen much of each other since she'd gotten on the school paper. She'd already made up her mind she was going to be a journalist, so when she looked me over I knew she was thinking as a reporter.

"You got a permanent," she observed. When I nodded she asked, "Why?"

That was one of the five words she'd told me were the first laws of journalism. A good reporter was supposed to find out, *who*, *what, where, when* and *why*.

"I just got tired of my hair stringing around my face," I told her.

Her dark eyes seemed to look right through me, and I was sure I hadn't fooled her a bit. She knew there was something more involved—probably a boy. But she was sensitive as well as sharp, and all she said was, "It looks great."

As soon as we turned in at the school, Mitch nudged me. I followed his glance and saw Ty on the front steps, a place that was practically reserved for upperclassmen. But with Ty, the football hero, you throw out the rules. Everyone was looking at him and listening to him, especially the girls. Gloria Putnam hung on his arm like a charm on a bracelet.

"Come on, let's go into our act," Mitch whispered.

Somehow he managed to shake the kids we were with, and at the foot of the stairs he slipped his arm around my waist. Bending over, he looked into my face, and from his expression you would have thought he was saying something romantic, instead of reciting the Gettysburg Address.

Oh, this was so silly! It was never going to work. Ty wouldn't pay the slightest attention to us no matter how we carried on. We were just an ordinary couple, bit players in a cast of hundreds, while he and Gloria—or some other spectacular girl—were the stars of Bayside High.

I had just enough confidence left in my scheme to give a toss of my head as we reached Ty, and to let one of my carefully rehearsed laughs ring out.

"Oh, Mitch!" I said in a voice the whole group had to hear. "You shouldn't say things like that! There are people around." He was onto the end of the Gettysburg Address now, and I felt like a traitor to Abraham Lincoln, but then I crossed my fingers so it wouldn't count.

"How can I help it?" Mitch came back with a wicked chuckle which he broke off in the middle as if he'd just realized there were other people around. The next minute he "discovered" Ty and Gloria, a theatrical term I'd learned from Kim's mother.

"Hey, Rogers, how you doing?" he said, speaking so heartily anyone would have thought they were best friends. "Have a good weekend? Oh, you know Denise Dreyer, don't you? Denise, this is Ty Rogers."

"Yeah, sure," Ty mumbled. He turned his shining head to see who Denise Dreyer was, and for just a second I thought I saw a glimmer of interest in his bottomless dark eyes. "Hi," he said. Then he looked down at Gloria, smiling in a way that seemed to say, *Don't pay any attention to these people, and maybe they'll go away.*

Mitch gave my arm an urgent little squeeze, prodding me to take up on what he'd begun. At the moment I felt about as vivacious as one of the slugs in Mom's garden, but I'd gotten Mitch into this, and the least I could do was to hold up my end. I gave my head a wild toss, and tilted my chin at a neck-breaking angle to look into Ty's face although I saw now, with the two boys standing together, that he wasn't as tall as Mitch.

"Hello, Ty," I said, showing him a lot of teeth as Kim had told me to do. Then I greeted Gloria with a friendly "Hi." Finally, addressing them both, I said, "Nice day, isn't it?"

"Yeah, it sure is." I was surprised that Ty was such a mumbler, but he was looking more puzzled by the second, and I had the feeling he was trying to remember if I was one of the long line of girls he'd gone with since eighth grade.

Gloria responded to my friendly words with a frown. "The sun is hard on my skin," she complained. "I'm so fair." She looked up at Ty for confirmation, but Mitch had trapped him into a discussion of some football formation to prolong the encounter.

I didn't want him to overdo it, though, and I didn't want to overdo it myself. Before I tossed my head again, I tugged at Mitch's arm.

"We'd better get inside," I said in my new lilting voice. "If we're late to homeroom one more time, Mrs. Meade will throw the book at us." I laughed, hinting at where we'd been all those times we'd supposedly been tardy.

Mitch picked up my cue as if it were an easy ground ball. "You're right, Denise. We'd better get going." He beamed a wide smile at Ty and Gloria. "We'll see you two around."

"Yeah, sure." Ty was muttering now.

Gloria muttered something, too, but I couldn't make out the words. They sounded a little like *not if we see you first.*

I didn't get a chance to talk to Kim until the middle of the morning when we had English together.

"You look fabulous!" she raved when she caught up with me outside the door. "Your hair looks even better today. And that skirt shows just the right amount of leg."

I didn't know if she was admiring me, or the job she'd done on me, but I thanked her before saying we'd better get into class. I was fighting for my life in English. I liked to read, and I liked words. Sometimes I'd even look up a word in the dictionary that I didn't have to. But grammar was something else.

Kim pulled me away from the door. "Tell me what happened! I saw you and Mitch leave for school together. Did you see Ty? Did he see you and Mitch—together?"

I told her about the scene on the front steps. "I don't think Ty was a bit impressed, but Mitch says it will sink in gradually, and the next time Ty sees me he'll really notice me."

"I'd bet Mitch is right." She looked at me closely. "You don't seem very thrilled, though. You know, you've already made a lot of progress. Ty knows you're alive. He didn't before."

I knew I'd spill out my feelings to her sooner or later, so I decided I might as well do it now. "I had the feeling Mitch was pushing me at Ty, and I didn't like it. I want him to help me, but—" I made a helpless gesture. "I can't explain how I feel."

Kim rolled her eyes toward the ceiling as if appealing for patience. "Do I have to be your psychologist as well as your fashion advisor?" I recognize a rhetorical question when I hear one, so I didn't bother to answer. "This is the way I see it. Deep down you'd like to feel that you're attractive to all boys, whether you're interested in them or not. You like Mitch only as a friend, but it hurts your ego to have him *push* you at another guy. Well, Denise Dreyer, you'd better make up your mind what you really want. You can't have it both ways. There! A psychologist couldn't give you any better advice."

"Send me a bill," I quipped. Not that I didn't take what she said seriously. Her dad was a general practitioner, not a psychologist, but he had a lot of psychology books, and I knew she read them—those that weren't under lock and key.

English passed without Miss Pritchard asking me any tricky questions about *who* or *whom*, or dangling participles. After that, study period was all I had before lunch.

I thought Mitch would have lunch with the guys like he always did, and that I'd sit with Kim and Carol and some of my other friends. At the cafeteria door, though, Mitch caught my arm and led me to the line. Kim was right—it was nice standing in the cafeteria as if we were boyfriend and girlfriend, but when I caught sight of Ty across the room, I knew that he was the one I wanted and I wished he was beside me in line. He was sitting at a table with Gloria, and that lock of glossy dark hair fell across his forehead, just so. He leaned forward as she talked, following the movement of her lips with rapt attention. Mitch could pick me up and throw me bodily at Ty if he would only look at me like that.

Mitch was watching them, too. "I wonder what she's whining about now," he said.

"'My skin is so fair,'" he mimicked in a falsetto voice. Then in his own voice he said, "One thing about you, Denny—you're not a whiner."

"Gee, thanks," I said.

Mitch led me to two empty seats away from everyone else. "We want to be conspicuous, and you can't be in a crowd," he pointed out.

I'd thought I would have to push and prod Mitch to get him to act as if he were in love with me, but he continued to lead the way. He fed me a bite of his cottage cheese, then, of course, I fed him a bite of my potato salad. He leaned across the table the way Ty had, and from his expression anyone would have thought he was whispering love words to me. Actually he was telling me the latest price of aluminum, and saying we'd soon have enough cans to take them to the salvage yard.

"Ty is looking over this way," he said after a minute. "Here, take a bite of my apple, and then I'll take a bite of it."

"Are you sure it doesn't have a worm in it?" This set us off laughing, and with all my head-tossing, and hand-waving, I was as vivacious as Kim could have wished.

After lunch break I had American history, which at the present time was my favorite subject because it was the only class I shared with Ty.

At first I hurried along in the hall, but

then I slowed down in case he should walk up beside me. If he had any notion of talking to me he'd forget it if I appeared to be rushing. When I reached the classroom I saw he was already in his seat. Luckily, I had to pass him to reach my own seat.

Or maybe it was unlucky. If I didn't follow up on what Mitch and I had started, the scene on the steps that morning would have been in vain. I didn't see how I *could* follow up, though, without Mitch beside me to give me moral support. I felt as nerdish as the girl at the curb that day when Ty had jumped out of the Camaro and grabbed Miriam's arm without even seeing me.

As I got close to Ty I noticed that Pete Jenkins, the guy who sat across from him, was looking at me in a way that boys had never looked at me before. With this proof that I was no longer that nerd by the curb, I became a bundle of vivacity.

"We meet again," I said gaily, pausing at Ty's desk.

"Huh?" He looked up from his book, blinked, then slowly focused his wonderful eyes on my face. "Oh, yeah, you're—Darleen."

I laughed, ignoring the fact that Mrs. Cole had just called the class to order. "I can never remember names, either. I'm Denise—you know, Mitch's friend."

"Oh, yeah, Mitch." He blinked again, but

this time when his eyes focused they became very busy, scanning my person from my autumn-leaf hair to the hem of my miniskirt and below.

I should say something, I thought. *But what? Or I should at least move to my seat.* I couldn't move, though. I felt frozen to the spot. Paralyzed. I felt as if I had stage fright, like Kim's mother gets sometimes. Then Mrs. Cole, who was famous for her sarcasm, brought down the curtain.

"Unless you're Betsy Ross and are about to demonstrate how you made the first flag, would you kindly take your seat, Miss Dreyer? As for you, Mr. Rogers, we're supposed to be studying American history here, not anatomy."

Almost everybody had been the victim of Mrs. Cole's biting wit at one time or another, and you wouldn't think they'd encourage her, but they—we—always did. As the hoots and hollers rang out I felt myself turn crimson. I would have crawled to my desk on my hands and knees if I hadn't feared that Mrs. Cole would make the situation worse by asking me if I'd lost something.

Once I was in my seat and the class had quieted down, I felt a little better. I could live with my own humiliation if I had to. But Ty wasn't used to anything but admiration and applause. He'd never forgive me for putting him in such a spot. *Why don't you leave me alone? I don't even know you,* I could hear him berating me if ever I had the nerve to speak to him again.

I slunk around school the rest of the day, hoping he wouldn't notice me, hoping no one would notice me. There were worse things than being invisible, as I told Kim when we walked home that afternoon. "Ty hates me now. I'm responsible for him being humiliated, and he'll always think of that, and feel sick, whenever he sees me. Which I hope will be never. I'm going to ask my folks tonight to send me to a private school."

"You know they won't. And don't be such a defeatist," Kim lectured me, using one of the terms I was sure she'd learned from her father's psychology books. "For one thing Mrs. Cole wouldn't have made that remark if Ty hadn't been admiring your anatomy. So you've reached your first goal. He's noticed you as an attractive girl."

"Well, yes," I had to agree. "But, still, everything's ruined between us, unless—," I broke off as a saving thought occurred to me. "Unless I apologize to him," I finished. "Yes, that's what I'll do!"

"Don't you dare," Kim said. "You'll really blow it if you do anything like that. Don't you see, that would only confirm his feelings of humiliation? The thing to do is to turn the whole episode into a joke. Laugh about it, and make him laugh. That's the only way he'll get over his embarrassment."

Kim knew a lot about boys, but this time I thought she was out in left field without a mitt. "Oh, sure, I just go up to him and say, 'ha, ha, wasn't that funny the way everybody got hysterical when Mrs. Cole called me Betsy Ross, and accused you of studying my anatomy in history class? Couldn't you just die laughing?'"

Kim gave me a hard stare. "I'm glad you have that out of your system. Now maybe we can get serious, and map out a scenario that will turn this thing around. We can talk it over when we get home. I have to get out of these shoes before I can think."

I couldn't help being glad that Kim's heels bothered her feet a little bit, too. I'd been afraid I'd ruined my arches by wearing sneakers all the time. "We'd better go to your place," I said. "Mom is roughing out her column today."

"Sure. We'll go to my place." Kim snapped at the suggestion like a hungry trout going for a fly. The only time my mother is temperamental is when she's doing the first draft of her column, at which time you'd think she was writing the Great American Novel. Kim's mother rehearsing Macbeth was a trip to Disneyland in comparison. Popping open a can of soda in my house was likely to call forth something like, "If you have to wreck the place would you please do it some other time?"

Kim unlocked the door of her split-level home. As we stepped into the hall, Mrs. Harris came from the living room to greet us. "Hello, girls. My, don't you look nice today, Denise."

I smiled, although I knew she hadn't noticed any change in me. She always said I looked nice. Besides, her mind was obviously on the script in her hand. "Well, have fun," she said, and drifted back into the living room. Kim and I headed for the kitchen.

"She's doing a new modern play," Kim whispered, "so we won't hear her even if she says her lines aloud. It's one of those things where everybody mumbles."

We got some sodas and chips and went up the half-flight of stairs to Kim's room. We sat on her bed; something my mother frowns on. Luckily, Mrs. Harris isn't into home-making in a serious way.

"Now," Kim said, pulling her feet into the lotus position, "we have to figure out some way to turn around what happened today so it will be a plus instead of a minus. Do you have any ideas?"

"Do I look as if I have any ideas?"

I guess I didn't because Kim went into a trancelike silence, finally coming out of it to say that the only approach she could think of was a little tricky, but it would work if I could pull it off.

"You go up to Ty tomorrow and say something like, 'Doesn't it break you up to think about what happened in history yesterday? One thing about Mrs. Cole, she only picks on the popular kids. She knows we can take it.'" Kim's eyes sparkled as she sold herself on the idea. "That turns it almost into a compliment! Ty will stop thinking about how embarrassed he was, and he'll end up laughing the whole thing off."

What she said about Mrs. Cole was usually true, but in my case it wasn't. "*I'm* not popular," I said.

"You are if you say you are."

Sometimes I think Kim spends too much time reading her dad's books. So, okay, maybe I could psych myself up to thinking I was one of Bayside's more popular girls, but could I sell Ty on the idea it was funny, and proof of our importance, that Mrs. Cole had picked on us?

I frowned over the matter for some time. It was tricky, as Kim had said, but if I put everything I had into it, I just might make it work. Ty would begin to see the incident as proof of his importance, and by extension, he'd begin to see me in the same rosy light.

"I'll give it a shot!" I finally told Kim.

Chapter 5

After dinner Mom and Dad and I settled down to watch the only TV program we all liked. When the phone rang, Mom went to answer it.

"It's for you, Denny," she said when she came back to the room. By her tone, I could tell that the call wasn't from Kim, or any other girl for that matter.

My heart took a wild leap that brought it halfway up to my throat. Could it possibly be Ty? Maybe he'd thought over what had happened in history that day, and had decided to warn me never to speak to him again . . . or maybe it was the opposite. He might have concluded we were fellow sufferers, and should stick together. *I just thought we might talk it over, Denise,* I could practically hear his low, rumbling voice in my ear.

As I ran to the hall Dad said to Mom, a mock grumble in his tone, "Well, I guess it's started, Laura. From now on if we want to make a call in the evening we'll have to have an appointment to use the phone."

Mom went along with his foolishness. "Patience, Neil, she'll be in college in a few years."

Dad would probably still be teasing me when walking me down the aisle to give me away—if I ever got married, which was a pretty big if.

"Hello." I spoke softly into the hall phone.

"Is that you, Denny? You don't sound like yourself."

"Oh, hello, Mitch." Naturally I couldn't tell him I didn't sound like myself because I'd been foolishly hoping the call was from Ty. "What's doing?" I said, raising my voice from a whisper to its normal, everyday pass-the-potatoes tone.

"I thought we did pretty well today," Mitch said. "Ty was really gawking at us in the cafeteria."

Ty does not gawk. He gives long glances of incredible depth and meaning. I kept the thought to myself and said, "Yeah, I guess we made an impression on him. Unfortunately, I made an even stronger impression on him later, and I may have blown the whole thing." I told him what had happened.

There was only a faint humming on the line for a minute, then Mitch said, "He can't blame you for that. All you did was stop and say a few words to him . . . but, hey, what was that stuff about anatomy? There are some ways a guy isn't supposed to look at a girl."

"Oh, Mitch!" I said, a little bit pleased that he was so defensive of my honor, and also a little bit annoyed because he wouldn't be much help to me if he took that attitude too far. "There was nothing wrong in the way he looked at me. After all, I bought some cute clothes so he would notice me. The point is," I went on, "that I may have struck out with him, unless Kim's idea works. Thanks to her I'll have another chance at bat." I explained.

"I don't know about all this acting, Denny . . . all this pretending. I've been thinking it over, and it seems to me that if you can't attract someone just being yourself, maybe they're not right for you."

The only reason I didn't scream into the phone was that I didn't want to shatter his eardrum. He'd been so great today, helping along my cause, and even though he seemed to be drawing back now I couldn't forget what he'd already done.

"We already talked about that," I reminded him, speaking in a quiet, reasonable tone. "Ty would never pay any attention to me if I were myself. That's what this whole thing is about. Later, when he gets to know me, I can cut out some of the—," I started to say *phoniness*, then thought better of it—"acting," I finished.

Mitch didn't comment. I hated it when he went silent on me.

"I'm going to school early tomorrow," he said finally. "I promised Coach Neff I'd help him check out the football equipment. So I guess I won't see you till later."

He was always helping with the equipment or helping the first-string players warm up or doing something for the team. It seemed to me that Coach Neff could show his appreciation by giving Mitch a little more playing time. He loved the game so much, and even though he wasn't flashy, like Ty, I was sure he could help win some games if he only got the chance.

"All right," I told him. "Thanks for calling, and thanks for helping me out like you did today."

Kim and I rode the bus the next morning. Carol was waiting at her corner, and she sat across the aisle from us.

"Got any hot items for me?" she asked. "I've been assigned to do a gossip column for the *Bayside Bugle.* Isn't that something for a future Pulitzer Prize winner?" she added sarcastically. "But the editor has spoken."

"You mean John Lerner?" I asked.

She gave me a withering glance. "I think it's pretty well known around school that John Lerener is the editor of the *Bugle*."

I had a habit of making small talk, responding in some way to everything that was said, or just dropping a few words into any silence that developed. Carol, as a student of writing, despised unnecessary words. I didn't hold it against her because I hated sloppy play on the soccer field.

"Sorry," I told her. "I'm afraid I don't have anything for you." Kim said she didn't, either.

Carol shrugged. She was really the last person in the world who should have to write a gossip column. She cared less than any girl I knew about who was going with whom.

"Before the term is over," she said, "I'm going to write a real story for the *Bugle*. It'll be so important John will have to publish it. Then he can find himself another reporter to write about who had sodas together at The Last Straw."

"Speaking of gossip," Kim said, "everybody seems to think Linda Smith and Joel Pierce are going to be the sweethearts of the Christmas Ball this year. You know anything about that, Carol?"

"It's more than a rumor. The committee

isn't ready to announce it yet, but it's in the bag," Carol told us. "Linda and Joel have all the qualifications—he's a senior, and she's a junior, and you know upperclassmen are nearly always picked." Kim and I nodded our heads, feeling privileged to be in on the scoop. "Besides that, he's an athlete," Carol went on, "captain of the basketball team, and she's a cheerleader. They're both good-looking, and top students, and they're active in school affairs. They've been going together for a long time, too, and that means they really care for each other."

"They've had some big fights," Kim pointed out.

"That's because they're both strong-minded people. But they always get together again, and that means their love is really strong."

"I guess," Kim agreed. Her eyes took on a faraway look now, and I knew she'd use the dance as an excuse to get a gorgeous new dress. She'd go with Randy, of course.

And I'll go with Ty. I had to believe that.

When we got off the bus Carol made a dash for the *Bugle* office at the back of the building. Kim headed for the front door, me right beside her. Then I saw Ty on the stairs, and I grabbed her arm.

"I'm going in the side door. I can't face Ty!"

She stared at me. "How about our plan? This is a perfect time to go up to him, with all those kids around. They'll all laugh along with you and Ty when you pull your line about Mrs. Cole only picking on the top kids."

I shook my head. "I can't. Not right now."

I must have looked as desperate as I felt because Kim nodded. "Okay, we'll go in the side door." I thought she'd probably noticed, as I had, how Ty was looking adoringly down at Gloria.

I'd wait till history for the big confrontation, I decided. It would be like returning to the scene of the crime. And at least, if he didn't react the way I hoped he would, no one else would hear. Besides that, history seemed a long way in the future. I had all kinds of classes before that. I even had lunch period. It would be practically a lifetime before I had to go up to him and act on Kim's wacky idea of pretending that the tragedy of yesterday had somehow turned into today's comedy.

The time came, though, and I was walking down the aisle in history as I had the day before. I paused at Ty's desk, my mouth so dry I wasn't sure I could speak.

"Hi!" My voice came out surprisingly strong and as bright as a robin's chirp. I tried a giggle, and that worked, too. Ty looked up, a scowl marring his perfect brow, but I tried not to notice. "Wasn't that funny yesterday?" I was practically choking on my laughter now. "Mrs. Cole can really be sarcastic, but she's kind of comical, too, and at least she only picks on the top kids. And I guess we can take it, can't we?"

First his brow smoothed out, then a smile began to tug at the corners of his faultless lips. It was uncertain at first—reluctant, really—but then it slowly broadened to a grin.

"Yeah, sure we can," he agreed, chuckling. "Cole isn't so bad, and like you say, she doesn't go after any of the wimpy kids."

"Well, listen," I said, flushed with victory, but not wanting to push my luck too far, "I'd better get to my seat before Cole starts on us again. See you, huh?"

"Sure. See you."

For the first time he made direct eye contact with me, and I felt as if I were drowning in the depths of his ebony gaze. I hurried to my seat before any mishaps could ruin my victory.

I couldn't wait to tell Kim how beautifully her idea had worked. And Mitch! He'd be pleased, too . . . or would he? I'd seen him at lunch and he'd asked if I'd talked to Ty yet. Reluctantly, I'd said I hadn't, thinking he'd accuse me of being chicken, but instead he just shrugged and walked away as if it were just as well. He had lunch with his best friend Keith Elliot and some other guys.

At the time I'd been a little bit worried at his indifference. What if he decided he didn't want to go on pretending to be my boyfriend? I couldn't go back to hanging around with other girls, or Ty would soon lose any interest he was beginning to have in me.

My worry came back now, but what kept me from being totally demoralized was the thought that Mitch had promised to see this through, and at least up until now his word had always been something you could take to the bank.

I made it through my other classes, then I went to phys ed, my last period. I was glad I was in the soccer section. That's my favorite sport, and today I felt as if I really needed to work off some steam.

"Hi," I said to Marie Logan. She was one of the transfer students that had come recently, and so far she seemed particularly unfriendly. But we were both late and the only two girls in the locker room, so I couldn't very well act as if she weren't there.

She said something that sounded as if she were gargling, then she turned her back on me and went to a far corner of the bench where she sat down and put on her shin guards and low soccer boots. All her stuff was top of the line—like the designer jeans and cashmere sweater she'd shoved in her locker as if they were rags.

My cheeks burned at the way she'd snubbed me. A lot of the transfers were unfriendly, but I'd never known one before to be that rude. We figured they were snobby because they moved all over the country, from the northeast to the southwest, and their parents were mostly big-shot engineers or scientists.

As I pulled on my jersey I watched Marie from the corner of my eye, and decided she was probably more snippy than the other transfers because she was so pretty— beautiful, really, with her perfect oval face and smooth black hair that fell almost to her waist. Usually she wore her hair pulled to the side, where it was held by a fancy comb. For soccer she wore it straight back and clasped at the nape of her neck. *Nobody* could wear their hair like that and still be gorgeous, but she managed to. The plain style only drew attention to her marvelous gray eyes.

I was glad to run out of the locker room and onto the field. The girls stood around in small groups waiting for Mrs. Frey to come out of the building. When I went up to the group they were talking about Marie.

"I don't think it's fair she should be on the team," Nancy Dolan was saying. "And a captain, of all things! Everyone knows the transfers don't have any school spirit. And Marie is the worst snob I've ever known. Yesterday I asked her if she'd help me with my dribbling—you know how well she does that, pushing the ball with one foot, then the other, without losing a second. Well"— Nancy's round face flushed an angry red— "she didn't even bother to answer me. She just walked away with her head in the air . . . as if she weren't tall enough already. She makes me feel like a midget."

"Don't feel too bad about it," I told Nancy. "I just got the same treatment." I don't know what made me go on to say something in Marie's defense. Maybe it was because I detected some envy in Nancy's complaint, or maybe it was because Marie was so alone. Even if she did ask for it, I hated to see everyone gang up on her. "She really does deserve to be on the team," I argued, "because she plays so well—better than any of us."

Nancy and I had always been friends, but she looked daggers at me now. "You can stick up for her if you want to, but I'm never going to speak to her again."

Marie had come out by now and was standing by herself. I would have felt awful not having anyone to talk to, but you could see it didn't bother her. She seemed to be thousands of miles away . . . probably in some place like New York or Dallas.

"I'm glad I'm not on her team," Nancy muttered, looking at Marie. "I wouldn't play if she was my captain."

We weren't in a league yet because soccer was new to Bayside, but two intramural teams had been formed. I was the captain of the A's, and Marie captained the Zs. Those were the names Mrs. Frey had given us because she said that was how she wanted us to learn the game—from A to Z.

"All right, girls, let's play soccer!" She came running out on the field now, blowing her whistle and clapping her hands. She was young and peppy, and we all liked her even though she drove us hard. "Come on, come on, let's look alive!" She was trying to get us into the spirit of the game, but it happened that I didn't need any encouragement to put my whole heart into it.

There are some things that when you do them they feel right and good, as if you'd been born to do them. That's the way I felt about soccer. The first time I headed the ball perfectly I must have jumped three feet in the air, yelling with joy. There's only a small area on your forehead that's just right for making contact with the ball, and you can't flinch, although that's the natural thing to do. I'd never forget that first time when I put it all together.

Mrs. Frey blew the whistle again, and the

game started. I played like I was on fire. Marie played like a robot—perfectly, but without emotion. I think maybe I inspired my team more than she did hers because the A's won more often than the Zs, and we won again that afternoon for my second victory of the day.

"How was school?" Mom asked. She was in the kitchen, and from the stuff I saw scattered on the drainboard I knew we were in for one of her culinary experiments. Over the weekend she usually gave us a break, cooking a roast or chicken or some normal food. But during the week she tried out recipes she'd print in her column—to see if they didn't kill us.

I considered her question. How had school been? Well, let's see . . . I'd flirted with the top boy on campus that day and he'd ended up flirting back—almost. Mitch had acted funny and I wasn't sure why. My team had won the soccer match and I couldn't have been more thrilled if it was the World Cup. I'd gotten a B on an English test when I'd been afraid I'd flunk it.

"Um, it was okay," I answered Mom's question. I used to tell her everything, but sometimes now I couldn't seem to tell her anything.

"Do you have homework to do?"

"I'm going to do it after dinner. Kim's coming over then and we'll study together."

"Do you really get any studying done with the two of you?" Mom put on her reading glasses to consult the recipe book. "One tablespoon of shoyu," she told herself.

"Sure," I said. "What are you cooking?"

"Matsutake Dobin Mushi, only I don't have small earthenware teapots, so I'm using a casserole dish."

"East Indian?" I guessed.

"Japanese." She opened a can of chestnuts. "I don't see how you can study with someone else."

"It's easy. We help each other."

"And I suppose you'll have the radio on?"

"Naturally."

"I should think it would be distracting."

I'd given up a long time ago trying to close the generation gap, so I poured a glass of milk, grabbed a couple of oatmeal cookies, and went down the street to Mitch's.

Susie was shooting baskets—or trying to. "The ball won't go in," she whined when she saw me.

"Funny. It does for Magic Johnson."

She flashed her sudden grin that could be pretty blinding when the sun caught her braces. "I guess I just have to keep practicing, huh?"

"I guess you do. Is Mitch home?"

"Nope. He called and said he'd be late."

"Did he say why—or where he'd be?" There was an odd, tight feeling in my chest. Mitch usually let me in on his plans.

"Nope." Susie suddenly felt aggrieved. "He gets to do anything he wants to. I don't get to do nothing."

"Anything," I corrected absently. *Where could he be?* I hadn't seen him since noon, and he'd been acting pretty funny then. "I'm getting so I notice girls a lot," he'd told me last Saturday.

Susie was gawking up at me. "Are you and Mitch in love now?" she asked.

"Why don't you ask him?"

"I did, but he told me to mind my own bee's wax."

She wasn't my sister or I would have seconded the motion. "We're—real good friends," I answered carefully.

"But that isn't like being in love, is it?"

"Oh, I don't know. It's pretty close."

"Then I guess I'm in love with Jamie Banks, because we're friends."

Had I ever been twelve? I wondered. Yes, I had been, and I could just barely remember what a mystery everything in the world had been to me then.

"Just don't pick out your trousseau yet," I told her.

"What's a trousseau?"

I slammed the gate behind me so I could pretend I hadn't heard her.

* * *

Dad lifted the cover of the casserole and sniffed. "There's something mighty fragrant in here, but I can't make out what it is," he remarked.

"It may be the dashi. The recipe calls for two cups of it," Mom told him.

"Cantonese?" he guessed.

"Japanese," I informed him.

Dad tasted it and put an enraptured look on his face. "Delicious!"

I tasted, but didn't comment.

After dinner Dad went to his den to make some calls. He was an insurance broker, and some people could only be reached in the evening. When Kim came over, Mom said she'd take over my chores in the kitchen.

"Oh, there's some Matsutake Dobin Mushi left, Kim. Perhaps you'd like a taste of it."

"Thanks, Mrs. Dreyer, but I filled up on frankfurters and beans, and we had cherry cheesecake for dessert."

Sometimes I wished my mother was an amateur actress instead of the author of a homemaking column. Cherry cheesecake— wow! And not even an experimental one, but a gorgeous creation right out of the supermarket freezer.

Kim and I made ourselves comfortable on the cushions beside the windows. I'd already told her how it had gone with Ty that day, but she wanted to hear more.

"You're really sure you repaired the damage from yesterday?"

"As sure as I am that I'm sitting here. You should have seen his grin when I said Mrs. Cole only picked on the popular kids. It was dazzling."

"It would be," she said in a cryptic tone.

Something warned me not to ask her to explain herself. Instead, I told her how Mitch had acted at noon. "When I told him about Ty he just shrugged as if it weren't important, and walked away. I don't think he's very interested in helping me anymore."

Kim made a dismissive gesture. "Boys get moods, just like we do."

Mitch had never had moods before. I kept the thought to myself. "When I went by his place after school he wasn't home."

"So? There are a hundred places he could have been."

"He could have been with another girl!" I burst out.

Kim looked shocked for a minute, then she shook her head. "He wasn't with another girl. You have my word on it."

"How do you know?"

"I know boys, especially Mitch. In a way I know him better than you do." Again she sounded cryptic. And again I decided against questioning her.

We settled down to our homework. I had trouble concentrating, though, and not because of the rock beat that was coming from my portable stereo on the floor between us. I couldn't help wondering if I was being stupid, not wanting Mitch to fall in love with another girl. What was he supposed to do when Ty and I began to go around together? He was getting used to going with a girl, but then all of a sudden he'd have no one.

I would have taken quite a dislike to myself if I hadn't decided Kim had been right when she'd said a girl liked to think that all boys were capable of falling in love with her, even though she didn't love them. If Mitch really got interested in another girl I'd be happy for him . . . wouldn't I?

After a while I went downstairs and got some sodas, then Kim and I talked about the Christmas dance. She still had doubts that Linda Smith and Joel Pierce would be chosen as sweethearts of the ball.

"They quarrel more than any couple I know of who are supposed to be in love. I think it's a power struggle. Both of them are so superior they don't like to be topped by anyone."

"Could be," I said. Neither one of them went out for soccer, and besides, they were upperclassmen, so I'd hadn't paid much attention to them.

"Do you have any ideas about getting Ty to ask you out?" Kim asked.

"I made my move today," I told her. "Now the ball's in his court. If he doesn't lob it back in a day or two I'll think of something." I didn't tell her I was still worried about Mitch, and that I didn't feel like making any plans until I saw him the next day.

Pretty soon the lights blinked off for a second, then came on again. Kim and I both knew that was my dad's way of announcing curfew.

"I can take a hint," Kim said, putting on her shoes.

We got to our feet, and I walked her to the door. "Let me know how the ball bounces," she said in an undertone.

"Yeah." I knew she was talking about Ty. But I was thinking about Mitch and wondering what he'd have to say tomorrow.

Chapter 6

When I left the house the next morning I intended to take the bus to school, but I saw Mitch on the next block, starting out on foot, and I ran to catch up with him.

"Hey, Mitch, wait a minute, will you?"

If he were really mad at me, my hopes of getting anywhere with Ty were extinct, but that wasn't the reason I felt so anxious as I dashed down the street, my semi-heels feeling like nails I was driving into the pavement. My denim miniskirt was tight, too, and I could only hope the zipper that ran all the way down the front wouldn't give way.

For a minute I was nostalgic for the days of sneakers and jeans, and Mitch and me being pals instead of would-be sweethearts. In those days he would have told me if something was bothering him, and if he hadn't I would have asked him right out what was eating him. Even when I caught up with him I couldn't seem to say what was on my mind.

"Hi," I said, giving him a half-flirty smile even though there was no one around to see it.

"Hi," he said in a tone that told me nothing. "Where's Kim?"

For some reason, I resented him asking me where Kim was, especially when I wanted to talk about us. He knew I was worried about something, so why didn't he ask me what was wrong?

"I guess she took the bus. You know she's no hiker."

"Yeah."

He was still dressing up more than he used to. This morning he wore honey-colored cords with a bulky brown sweater over a blue shirt. He still started out with his hair combed back, too, but it naturally fell into bangs, and they already tumbled over his forehead. They gave him sort of a shaggy-bear look that I supposed a lot of girls would think was cute. Suddenly I was sure he'd been with a girl the day before.

"I went by your house yesterday," I said. "Did Sue tell you?"

"No. She only talks when you don't want her to." He gave a little smile, and even though it was Susie that inspired it, I felt slightly encouraged.

"She told me you were out. She didn't know where."

"That's because I didn't tell her."

This was ridiculous! Mitch and I didn't keep secrets from each other. I was going to put an end to it even if I wrecked my whole scheme to get Ty interested in me. I stopped and grabbed Mitch's arm.

"What's going on here, Mitch Conley? Yesterday when I told you I hadn't pulled that trick on Ty yet—acting like what Mrs. Cole said to us was a big joke—you didn't seem to care one way or the other. You just shrugged and walked away, and had lunch with your friends. Then after school you went off some place and you won't tell me where. And now you're mad about something. You haven't even looked at me this morning."

"I'm not mad!" Mitch denied. "Why should I be?" But his eyes still didn't meet mine.

"If you're not mad why don't you look at me? And why won't you tell me where you were yesterday afternoon?" I hated how shrill my voice sounded, but I'd never been so upset with him.

"I wasn't anywhere," he muttered. "I—just biked out to the country the way we used to do. I wanted to be alone."

"Then everything is all right between us?" I asked on a big sigh of relief. What I really meant was—*then you weren't with another girl.*

"Sure it is. But, Denny—about you and Ty . . ."

He was looking at me now, right into my eyes, and I'd never seen his eyes so dark and stormy. My heart beat fast as I wondered if he had some special reason for being troubled because I wanted to go out with Ty. I knew how I'd felt when I thought he might have gone out with another girl. Being good friends could make a person feel possessive toward another person. Did Mitch feel that way about me? Was he beginning to get jealous of Ty?

All at once he gave a little smile. "I've been wondering if that trick you pulled on Ty yesterday worked. You went through with it, didn't you?"

I laughed. "He loved it when I pointed out that Mrs. Cole only picked on the top kids, like me and him."

Mitch blinked. "He *did*? You know, a person would have to have an ego the size of Texas—" He caught his breath, looking at me as if he thought I'd be mad, but I laughed again.

"Ty does have a giant-sized ego. That's the whole idea. There's nothing wrong with it— it's just the way some people are." *It's why they're number one at what they do.* "He just smiled at me, and that was it."

"Umm." He turned around and began walking again. "How's soccer?" he asked abruptly.

"Fine. We beat the Zs yesterday. That transfer Marie Logan is their captain."

"You mean the girl whose mother picks her up in the Cadillac Seville with the Texas plates?"

Mitch was inclined to identify people by the cars they drove or rode in. "Probably," I said. "I haven't noticed the kind of car her mother drives, but I'm sure it's a big expensive one."

"We have a transfer on the football team. Nobody likes him much. He acts like he's better than anyone, probably because his dad's a big-wheel engineer."

"They do act snobby," I agreed.

We didn't say anything for a minute, then Mitch said, "Speaking of football, Coach Neff is working with me on my passing. He says I have the right stuff to be a good quarterback if I could only learn to move around in the pocket more."

"You would be," I encouraged him. "You'd be great!"

We caught up with some other kids then, and there was a lot of laughing and talking. When we got to school, though, Mitch and I broke away from the others as we had before.

"Time to go into our act," he said as soon

as we were alone. He took my hand, and
because we were a little early we strolled
around the campus. Every now and then
he'd lean over as if he were whispering
something sweet and confidential in my ear.
Even though he was only repeating the
weather report that had come over the radio
that morning he made it look good. I was so
thrilled that everything was right between
us again, and that he was still willing to
help me, that I played my part to the hilt. I
gazed up into his eyes, and I smiled softly,
fanning my lashes that were surprisingly
long and thick with the touch of mascara
I applied to them these days. Once he
touched my hair, and a minute later I
stroked his jaw. It was kind of fuzzy. Before
long he'd have to start shaving.

When it was finally time to go inside, we
walked up the stairs, still hand in hand. Ty
was standing there with his usual admiring
circle around him, including Gloria, who
appeared to be stapled to his arm. Mitch
nodded to Ty, but then acted as if he were
too absorbed in me to pause. I took my cue
from him and smiled dreamily. Ty had no
way of knowing he was the one I was
dreaming about. I could only hope his competitive spirit made him wish he was.

That afternoon as Kim and I waited for the
bus, she told me *everyone* had been watch-

ing Mitch and me that day. "The kids think
you've got a big romance going."

"I know one person who doesn't care if I
elope with Mitch," I said. "Ty didn't even
look up from his book when I walked past
him in history."

"Don't worry. All this talk is bound to
make an impression on him," Kim insisted.
"He's the kind who'd like to break up a
couple who were really serious about each
other."

I didn't like the way she made that sound.
"We already agreed he'd only be interested in
me if I was going with another boy. It's his
competitive nature, so you don't have to
make it sound as if he had a major charac-
ter flaw," I said sharply.

"Whatever you say."

I didn't like the way that sounded, either,
like she was humoring me, but I let it go. I
told her about Coach Neff working with
Mitch. "Wouldn't it be great if Mitch got to
play a few minutes in the big game? If the
Cougars get far enough ahead, the coach
may rest Ty for a while."

The big game was to be played the Saturday afternoon before Thanksgiving, and
that wasn't far away. The Cougars would
play the Eagles of Valley View, and the
winner would be the champion of the
league.

"I know Mitch would be a great quarterback. I only hope he gets the chance to show his stuff," Kim remarked. "Hey, how about going to the mall this afternoon?"

At one time I would have groaned, but no more. "I could use a new dress for Friday," I said.

"What's doing Friday?"

I told her my latest brainstorm. "You know how a lot of the kids dress up on Friday, and go to The Last Straw. It's almost like a party." She nodded. "Well, I'm going to ask Mitch to go with me this Friday. Ty and Gloria will probably be there, and the way everyone circulates and talks to everyone else, it'll be a good chance for me to get acquainted with Ty."

"You haven't asked Mitch about it yet?"

"Well, no, but I know it'll be all right with him. He's getting so tired of all this pretending we've been doing he almost overdid the romance bit today. But he'll still do anything to help out."

"Umm," Kim said thoughtfully. There were times lately when I couldn't guess what was on her mind.

I found my dress staring at me from the window of a department store at the mall. It was a silky green shirtwaist that would be sensational if it were jazzed up with some striking gold jewelry. I didn't happen to have any gold jewelry, striking or otherwise, and if I bought the dress I'd be stretching my credit to the breaking point and beyond. Luckily I had a good friend.

"You know that heavy gold chain you have, and the gold hoops?" I asked Kim.

"Yes. What about them?" She played dumb for a minute, but then she couldn't keep a straight face. "Don't look so agonized. You can pick them up when we get home."

Mom was in the kitchen when I went in the house. I didn't smell anything suspicious, so maybe we were going to be lucky tonight.

"I bought a dress," I announced. I didn't dare take off the price tag until she approved the purchase. "Isn't it gorgeous?" I held it up for her inspection.

"Lovely," she said, then looked at the ticket. From the way she frowned I was afraid she was going to make me take it back, and I felt my tear ducts getting ready for action. In the end, though, she only said "Umm." I sighed with relief.

It turned out she wasn't through, however. "For the sake of the family credit rating I think you'd better give me back the little plastic card I loaned you when you went on your recent shopping spree." She was already holding out her hand.

"Oh, fine," I grumbled. "My credit was good as long as I didn't use it." I grinned to let her know I was joking, and she grinned back.

"You'll find throughout life," she told me, "that that's the way credit works. You can get all you want as long as you don't need it."

I felt as if I were giving up a newfound but very dear friend as I surrendered the tiny bit of plastic. I only hoped the price of aluminum held up, and that the rainy season didn't come too soon so that Mitch and I could go on collecting cans. I needed money more than ever now, and that was my only means of earning any. Most of the people in our neighborhood were about the same age as my parents, and a lot more girls were looking for baby-sitting jobs than there were babies to go around.

After dinner I called Mitch. When I told him my idea about going to The Last Straw he said, "Gee, I'm sorry, Denny, but I'd planned on practicing Friday afternoon. Coach promised to stay and work with me."

"Oh, well, then . . ." It took me only a second to rally, and make out as if it really weren't important. But even over the phone Mitch could read me.

"Listen, if I put in some extra time the next couple of days it'll be all right. Sure, we'll go to The Straw on Friday. It's a great place for us to show how crazy we are about each other. Let Ty Rogers eat his heart out."

I almost died at the thought of Ty eating his heart out over me, but I still managed to say, "No, Mitch, you go ahead and practice, like you planned." The next time I looked in the mirror I didn't want to see a girl I hated.

"Make up your mind, woman," Mitch gave one of his mock growls. "You want to go to The Straw, or don't you?"

"I . . . guess I do," I said weakly. I'd tell the girl in the mirror I knew there were extenuating circumstances for her selfish behavior.

"Okay. I'll meet you out front after school."

"Kim and Randy are going, too, so we can make it a foursome." I was getting more excited by the minute.

"Now if Ty shows up you'll have it made." Mitch still spoke in a growling sort of tone, but maybe his voice was just getting deeper, I thought.

"I bet anything he will," I said. "He goes to the Straw almost every Friday when there's no football practice. Gloria will probably be with him, but at least he'll see me, and with any luck we'll speak a few words. I—I have a pretty new dress." The thought of it made me breathless.

"You're pretty, too."

The words were so mumbled I wasn't sure if I'd really heard them. And the next minute, Mitch said he'd better hang up and hit the books.

I should have done some studying, too, but I was too excited to even open a book. My closet drew me, and I finally decided I might as well do what I'd been dying to do ever since I got home. I put on my new dress, then going all out, I added Kim's heavy gold chain and big matching ear hoops.

"Ty *has* to be impressed," I decided aloud. I'd just struck a model's pose when Mom knocked on the door.

"May I come in, Denny? I ironed some of your blouses today."

I threw open the door. "Oh, Mom, I'm sorry! I meant to iron them."

"Good intentions don't empty my ironing basket," she said. When I'd hung up my blouses she focused on my dress and jewelry. "Aren't you just a teensy bit dressed up for an evening of homework?"

"I'm going to wear my new dress on Friday, and I wanted to be sure it looks okay." I whirled around so she could see how far her tomboy had come.

"It looks fine, but it seems to me it's too dressy for school, especially with the jewelry. Incidentally, if you charged all that gold you're going to be in debt well into the next century."

I explained that the jewelry was Kim's. "And I won't be too dressed up for Friday.

That's always sort of a party day. Mitch and I
are going to The Last Straw after school."

Mention Mitch to my mother these days
and she melts like a candy bar you forgot in
your pocket. She probably felt she had the
best of two worlds. Her daughter was dating, yet she had nothing to worry about
because she was going with a boy from
down the street who was as safe as a
brother.

I hated to take my dress off, but when
Mom had left I finally did. As I put it away on
a padded hanger I thought that Friday just
might be the biggest day of my life.

Chapter 7

The Last Straw had been the school hangout for as long as anyone could remember. Everything happened there. Couples got together or broke up. There was flirting and sometimes a fight. If a boy and girl went together a few times everyone figured it was serious between them.

"There's a booth!" Kim said as she and Randy led the way inside.

"Let's grab it!" I pulled Mitch along by the hand. He seemed to feel kind of uncertain about this double dating, as if he might be venturing into deeper water than was safe.

Kim and I slid onto the benches while the boys went to get sodas and french fries. "Isn't this great?" I said. Kim nodded in vigorous agreement.

Only couples were supposed to take the booths. There was no rule about it, it just worked that way. Other kids sat on the stools, or at tables out in the middle of the room. I'd been here lots of times before with other girls, but for the first time I felt as if I really belonged.

Randy didn't know what was up, of course, so when he and Mitch came back he acted like we were on a double date.

"I want you and Denny to come hear me play some night," he told Mitch. "Kim can go with you, and later we can come here, or something. I do some school gigs, and stuff like that, all up and down the peninsula."

"Yeah, sure—that sounds good," Mitch said. He was beaming by now, and not a minute too soon, because just then the door opened and Ty and Gloria walked in.

I could have hugged Mitch when he jumped up and called out, "Hi, Gloria, Rogers, you guys want to join us?"

I wondered if Ty would ever stop looking puzzled when Mitch or I spoke to him. "Well—," he said. He looked around hopefully, but the place was jammed. There wasn't a booth available. He and his date would have to sit at the counter if he didn't accept Mitch's invitation. "I'll get some sodas and stuff," he mumbled.

Before he went to the counter he scowled at Gloria. "If you hadn't spent a half hour combing your hair, or whatever you were doing in the rest room, we could have had our own booth," he told her in a grating voice.

I wouldn't have put up with that from a boy, but I supposed that's the way it was when a couple didn't belong together. They'd naturally get on each other's nerves.

"I had to mousse my hair three times before I could do anything with it," Gloria complained. "My hair is so fine," she confided to the table at large.

Ty went to the counter and came back with sodas and french fries. Gloria tasted one of the fries and made a face. "They're greasy," she said.

Ty frowned but didn't say anything. Neither did anyone else for quite a while. There was a mirror beside the booth, and Gloria became absorbed admiring herself. Randy rapped his knuckles on the table, drumming out the soft beat that came from the stereo. The middle-aged manager hated the hard stuff and had the stereo up on the wall so no one could reach it. Randy wore jeans and an old denim jacket over a T-shirt. His hair was too long, and his face was thin, but nice-looking in kind of a soulful way. Kim swayed to the music.

I looked at Ty, although I tried not to be too obvious about it. He was so good to look at I would have paid admission. He had a little mole high on his left cheek that was like a fleck of gold against his perfect skin. His mouth had a discontented droop at the moment, but it was so beautifully shaped that it didn't seem to matter. Most people's noses are good only for breathing, but his was like an ornament on his face, straight and noble.

Finally Mitch slurped his soda. "Why don't you get another one?" I suggested sweetly. His slurping had bugged me even when he was eight.

"Don't want another one. Just wanted to be sure I got all of that one." That was the same thing he'd said then. I was getting ready to tromp on his foot when he spoke to Ty in the special, hearty tone he'd developed for him. I knew he didn't like Ty very much, but by being friendly with him he was giving me a better shot at attracting his attention.

"You think the Cougars are going to win the big game this year?" he asked.

Ty gave a snort. "Unless I break my right arm before then. It's just a question of how big a score we run up on them." He made a move with his arm as if he were getting off a long pass, and I could almost feel the energy he put into his game.

"How big a score do you think the Cougars will run up?" I asked.

"Are you girls football fans?" Although I was the one who'd spoken, Ty looked at Kim.

"I go to some of the games," she answered, "mostly because Denise drags me to them.

She's the fan." As she spoke she slipped her hand into Randy's. "I'm more interested in music." She turned away from Ty to smile at Randy.

I'd sometimes wondered why Ty had never tried to date Kim, considering how pretty she was. Now I knew. He'd sensed that she'd turn him down.

"So you're the big fan," Ty said, finally looking at me.

"Oh, yes, I go to all the games!" I was so excited I could hardly speak.

"I haven't noticed you." He gave me another one of those puzzled glances.

Of course he hadn't noticed me with all those gorgeous cheerleaders prancing around on the sidelines. But I had a chance to make him notice me now and I jumped at it with both feet.

"I just love football!" I enthused. "It's such a beautiful game, with all the running and jumping, but most of all, the passing."

Ty seemed to forget there was anyone else at the table. He leaned forward, talking just to me. "I really dig a girl who likes football," he said. "I tell you what, D . . . Denise . . . I'm going to dedicate my first touchdown pass in the big game to you."

"Oh!" I gasped. I was so flushed I felt as if I had a temperature of 104. It was plain we'd reached a new point in our relationship. He'd never be confused again about who I was and how we happened to be talking. I doubted if he'd ever stumble over my name again.

My gasp seemed to wake Gloria up to the fact that something was going on. She gave a last loving glance at her reflection before tuning from the mirror.

"Let's go," she whined to Ty. "This place is no fun if we don't have our own booth."

Ty frowned but got slowly and gracefully to his feet. Just before they moved away he gave me his thousand-watt smile.

"Remember, my first pass in the big game has your name on it."

Saturday it seemed funny to be collecting cans again. After the miracle of Friday afternoon at The Straw it seemed to me as if the whole world had changed. I should be wearing a pair of glass slippers instead of grungy old sneakers. Still, I needed money more than ever, and besides, I couldn't very well let Mitch down when he'd been responsible for the miracle.

"Want to try the beach today?" he asked.

The peninsula is divided by a low range of mountains. The Pacific Ocean is on one side, and on the other is San Francisco Bay. I knew Mitch was referring to the beach on the bay side, which was only a short distance away, and easy biking.

"Sure," I said.

The pickings were pretty good—or pretty bad from a trash pollution viewpoint—so we filled our bags shortly before noon. We'd brought lunch, not knowing we'd be so lucky, so we decided to have a picnic.

"Let's sit here," Mitch said, thumping a piece of driftwood to be sure it was solid enough to use as a backrest. The sand was a little bit damp but we sat down and unwrapped our sandwiches.

"What kind you got?" Mitch asked.

"Cheese."

"You always have cheese."

"What kind have you got?"

"Ham."

"You always have ham."

"Want to go halves?" he asked.

"Sure."

It wasn't exciting to be with Mitch but it sure was relaxing. With Ty I got chills and fever. Mitch was like a warm blanket. We didn't say anything while we ate . . . just watched the sea gulls wheeling in a sky that was as blue as a robin's egg except for some little white clouds that drifted overhead now and then.

"That one looks like a camel," I said after a while.

"Yeah." Mitch didn't have to ask what I was talking about. We'd always seen animal shapes in the clouds.

We finished the milk I'd brought in a thermos. Mitch got a white moustache. When I told him about it, he wiped it away with the back of his hand.

"Randy's a nice guy," he said. "He's really into music, isn't he?"

I nodded, then thinking of the day before, I put my hand on his arm. "You were great at The Straw," I said, "getting Ty to sit in our booth, then bringing up the subject of football so I could show him what a fan I am. I really think he's interested in me now. So maybe pretty soon we can start to cool our big romance." I laughed, but Mitch didn't join in.

"What are friends for?" My hand fell away from his arm as he stood up abruptly. "Let's hit the road," he said.

As we started home, the clouds got darker. "You think it's going to rain?" I asked.

"Probably. It's November now . . . So I guess we won't be collecting cans many more times this year." He turned his head to look at me. "It was kind of fun, wasn't it?" He sounded sad that it was almost over.

"Yeah," I said. I felt the same way.

Monday I got to history early so I'd be sure to catch Ty before he went into the room. I stood in the hall just outside the door, leaning against the wall and pretending to do some last-minute cramming while keeping one eye out for Ty. When I saw him coming, I lazily straightened up.

"Oh, hi," I said, as if I'd just seen him. Indicating my book, I laughed. "I didn't get a bit of studying done over the weekend. You know how it is."

"I sure do." He got a dreamy look in his eyes, and I knew it wasn't for me so I quickly went on.

"I hope you haven't forgotten your promise to dedicate your first touchdown pass to me." I tipped my head way back, as if he were seven feet tall, and gave him my brightest smile.

For a minute he looked as if he had forgotten his promise, but then he said, "Oh, no. The first one's yours."

"I wonder how many you'll get."

"It's hard to say, but I expect to run up a pretty big score on the Eagles. They do have a good team this year, but not good enough to beat us."

He expected to run up a big score. *So, okay,* I told myself. *Mitch is a team player and what's it gotten him?* "It's amazing how you maneuver around in the pocket," I told Ty.

He was really responding to me now, his eyes glowing as they looked into mine. "That's what makes a great quarterback."

"I play soccer," I said eagerly. "It's a great game, too."

"I suppose." He began to back toward the door.

I couldn't let him go, now that we were really talking, just the two of us. "Soccer's really a form of football," I rushed on, babbling the first thoughts that came to mind just to keep talking. "It originated in England a long time ago. The ball was handled in those days, but some people thought it would be better just to kick, or head it, so—"

Even though I was talking as fast as I could and tossing my head and making a lot of gestures, just as Kim had instructed, Ty had lost interest. First his eyes went blank, then they glazed over. I could throw in the second act of Hamlet and he'd still back away. I'd lost him when I'd stopped talking about *his* game and started to talk about my own.

"I can hardly wait for the big football game. Only a few more days now," I said frantically. But it was too late. The bell had rung.

That afternoon my team beat Marie's once again. "Nice game," she said, and gave me the traditional handshake. She always observed the rules of sportsmanship, and I had to admire her for that.

I showered and dressed as quickly as I could, and hurried toward the bus stop. I was halfway there when I realized I'd left my books in the locker room. I ran back as fast as I could and grabbed them up from the bench. Everyone was gone, or at least I thought they were. Then I heard a sound, like someone crying. I looked around, and there was Marie, leaning against her locker, trying hard to muffle her sobs.

"Marie?" I said.

"Go away!" she sniffled.

I paid no attention. "Is there anything I can do to help?"

"No." She drew herself up as proudly as ever, even though her eyes were swollen and her nose red. "How can you help me when the best allergists in the country can't?"

I'd seen people with allergy, and I'd seen people crying, and I thought I knew the difference. "There's nothing wrong with crying," I said. "Other girls cry. Boys, too."

All of a sudden Marie gave a big sob. "I just can't help it!" she wailed, as if she had to apologize. "I get so lonely sometimes."

She sank down on a bench, and I sat beside her. "You sure haven't acted lonely," I reminded her. "I tried to be friendly at first, but—"

She shook her head. "You don't understand. I had to act mean because I was beginning to like you."

If that was an explanation, it was the craziest one I'd ever heard. Marie took a deep breath to steady herself. "If you and I become friends, I'll only end up getting hurt, because I'll only move away again." In a rush of words she told me how difficult it was. "We're never invited to hold class office, or to join a club. This is the first time I've ever been on a team."

She stood up suddenly. "Please forget we ever had this conversation. I don't know what got into me. I like things just the way they are."

I opened my mouth to say something more, but it was plain she didn't want to talk to anyone. She was staring over my head.

I grabbed my books and ran, but I'd missed the bus. I was plodding home when Carol yelled at me to wait for her. When she caught up with me she told me John, her editor, had kept her late.

"He has me doing just about everything but sweeping the floor," she grumbled. "But will he give me a chance to write a serious article? No!"

"That's too bad," I said, so full of Marie's problem I'd barely heard what Carol had said.

"A lot you care," she snapped. "You weren't even listening!"

The trouble with knowing people all your life is that you can't fool them. I told Carol I was sorry, and as an excuse for not being more concerned I spilled out the conversation I'd just had with Marie.

"Those poor kids really have it rough. They can never make friends. They never have a school that's theirs. They never get to belong to a club, or—"

Carol had suddenly grabbed my arm. Her eyes were wildly excited behind her big, unfashionable glasses. "That's my feature article!" she cried.

I shook off her arm. "Don't you dare write an article about Marie!" I told her. "She'd never trust anyone again for the rest of her life."

"I won't mention her name—or yours, if you don't want me to, but I have to write this story, Denny. Think of the good it could do. I'll make everyone see how lonely these kids are, and how unfair we've been to them. I even have a solution to their problem. We could organize a welcoming committee to meet them when they report to the registration office. . . ."

She went on and on, and I finally began to see that she did have a good idea. I just warned her again not to print my name or Marie's. I hoped Marie would think the article had nothing to do with what she'd told me.

When I got home, Mom's car was in the garage, but she wasn't in the house, which meant she was out in her potting shed. I ran up to my room and dialed Kim's number. No answer. Darn! She and her mom had probably gone to the mall. When Dr. Harris had a staff meeting at night they sometimes went shopping and had dinner at the mall. I was dying to talk to Kim about my conversation with Ty that day. I'd learned a lot from it and I was anxious to talk it over with her.

After this I won't bore him by talking about soccer. I'll ask him what rock groups he likes, and what kind of books and movies he enjoys. Until we really get acquainted I won't talk too much about myself and what I like.

I went downstairs, gulped a glass of milk, and went out to the backyard.

"I'm here, Denny!" Mom called from the potting shed.

Somehow she always managed to look immaculate, even though she was up to her elbows in potting soil. Right now she had African violets spread all over the place, from single leaves to full plants.

"So many of my readers have trouble with their African violets." She seemed to be at a critical stage in starting a leaf, and she didn't look up. "They can't seem to keep them blooming, so I'm experimenting, trying to produce a foolproof variety. Not that my readers are fools, but the plant originally comes from a hot, very humid climate, so getting them to bloom well here takes some doing."

Finally she said, "There, we'll just leave this little fellow alone for a while and see how well he does." She looked at me now. "How was your day, dear?" Her smile almost made me forget that she asked the same question every day. I told her about Marie, and the article Carol was going to write. She gave me a hug, potting soil and all. "That's beautiful, Denny! I'm so glad you drew that poor girl out, and I hope Carol's idea of a welcoming committee catches on."

That night at dinner she told Dad the whole story, and he beamed at me. It was nice to bask in their approval but I could still hardly wait to talk to Kim. As soon as we left the table I began to watch across the street for her light to go on. When it did I ran up to my room and called her.

First I told her about my conversation with Marie, and the article Carol was going to write. She thought that was great. Next I told her about my exchange with Ty, but for some reason I changed it a little bit. I didn't tell her how bored he'd been when I'd talked about soccer. I just said we'd talked, and he'd repeated that he was going to dedicate a touchdown to me.

"Nice going, Denny." Then out of nowhere she said, "Mitch is sure a neat kid."

I'd always known he was a neat kid, and I kind of resented the fact that she felt she had to remind me of it. "Well, it's getting late," I said. "I guess we'd better go."

When I hung up I took Ty's picture from my diary, and for the first time I kissed his lips . . . very softly.

"Good night, sweet prince."

Chapter 8

Carol's article titled: "Transfer Students—
Let's Give Them A Break" came out in the
Thursday edition of the *Bayside Bugle*.
Carol's story was on page one, and everyone
in school was excited about it.

"Gee, I never thought how awful it must
be for those kids," I heard one girl say.

Most of the comments I overheard were
about the same, although a few people said
it was the transfers' own fault because they
didn't even try to be friendly. Carol had kept
her word in not using Marie's name, and
since my name didn't appear in the article,
either, I hoped Marie would think it was a
coincidence that Carol had written it.

I got a big surprise when Gerri Carson, a
senior who was very prominent in school
affairs, called me out of study hall.

"There's a conference room down the hall where we can talk," Gerri told me.

"Talk about what?"

She had that remote, superior look most seniors have, and when she said she'd tell me in the conference room I didn't dare say any more.

There was no one else in the small conference room and Gerri and I took seats at the round table in the middle.

"We're starting a new committee here at Bayside," Gerri began at last, "to welcome the new transfer students. I've been asked to head the committee, and I'd like you to serve on it. It's only right you should because Carol says you inspired her article."

Thanks a lot, Carol, I thought. Still, I was glad Carol had mentioned my name to Gerri, and all of a sudden the idea of working on the committee kind of appealed to me. After my talk with Marie I really felt for those kids. I told Gerri I'd be glad to serve, and she said we'd have a full meeting within a few days.

I left school late that afternoon and missed Kim, but I called her the minute I got home. When I told her about the committee she was enthusiastic.

"Have you told Mitch about it yet?" she asked.

"Yeah, I stopped by his house on my way home from school." I laughed as I remembered how he'd blown the whole thing up. "He seemed to think this was the first step in me becoming a big school leader or something."

"Well, it was great that you got through to a girl like Marie," Kim said. Then abruptly she asked, "What did Ty say about it?"

"My goodness, I don't discuss everything that happens with Ty!" She knew Ty and I weren't that close, so why was she even asking?

"But you told Mitch," she persisted.

"Mitch and I are old friends."

"Oh," she said, somehow making it sound as if she was saying a lot more.

In soccer the next day Marie gave me a hard look, but I stared right back at her, and pretty soon a smile formed on her lips. When her team beat mine that day, and I went up to shake hands with her, her smile was more like a grin. "My girls really played their hearts out today," she said.

I was pretty sure that was because most of them had read Carol's article, and no longer resented their captain the way they used to. It really made me feel good that I had something to do with it.

That afternoon when I walked home with Mitch he asked if I'd like to go to the movies. "It's Friday night, and—maybe Ty will be there. That would give us a great chance to put on our act for him."

A real date?! I thought at first. For a minute I'd been kind of breathless; my first date! But no, we were just going out so Ty could see us together. I don't know why, but I felt kind of disappointed. So what if this isn't a real date, I told myself. Soon I'd be going out with Ty, and what could be better than that?

"Sure," I said. "Shall we leave around seven?"

As we walked to the Parkside that evening, Mitch grumbled, as he did at least twice a day, about how he wished he had a car.

"Wouldn't it be great if I could drive us?" he asked.

"You'll be driving before you know it," I said, which was a variation of what I always said. He wouldn't be sixteen for months, but I knew it made him feel good to just talk about driving.

Before we got to the theater I tried to give him the money for my ticket, but he wouldn't take it.

"That was our agreement," I reminded him. "When we go some place together it isn't supposed to cost you anything."

"Next time," he said. "This time's on me."

When he stuck his chin out like that it was no use to argue with him. He really shouldn't pay my way, though. It was too much like we were really dating, and we weren't. Next time I'd pay for both of us, I promised myself. When you dated a boy you felt different about him, and I wasn't supposed to feel that way about Mitch.

Almost everyone we knew was at the Parkside by the time we got there, standing in the ticket line, or just hanging around for a while before going inside. I didn't see Ty, though, even when I scanned the street in both directions. Finally Mitch and I went inside, and I had to give up.

I was disappointed for a while, then the movie started and I soon got caught up in it. Mitch got into it in the same way I did. When I went to the movies with Kim or some of the other girls, they did a lot of whispering that broke into my mood. Mitch and I just passed the popcorn back and forth and watched the screen.

As we walked home later Mitch came back to his favorite subject. "If I had a car we could drive to Crystal Springs Lake."

"I bet it's pretty up there in the moonlight," I said, for once dreaming along with him.

We talked about the different kinds of cars he was considering buying, and some of the different places we could go when he had wheels. After a while he took my hand. At first I felt funny—I mean, it was pretty doubtful that Ty would see us now—but then I decided that I liked Mitch's hand around mine, and it was good practice besides. We walked along that way until we got to my door. There we suddenly got awkward with each other. It was as if we'd been on a real date, and something special should happen.

"Well, thanks," I finally said. "I really enjoyed the movie." That sounded so stiff and formal. I wished more than ever that I'd paid my own way so I could just say good night and go inside.

"Me, too." Mitch shifted his feet. He'd dressed up in slacks and a sports jacket and real shoes. I figured the shoes were hurting his feet, he was so used to sneakers. I'd worn my little heels with a nice skirt and blouse, but I was used to leather shoes now so they didn't bother my feet anymore. It was too bad Ty hadn't been at the movie theater to see us looking so nice together, I thought fleetingly.

"I guess I should go in," I said.

"I suppose so," Mitch said, "but—" He shifted his weight back the other way.

The porch light was on, the way the folks used to leave it when Bonnie was dating. I noticed a moth flitting around it, and hoped it wouldn't burn its wings on the hot bulb.

"Denise."

Mitch spoke so suddenly I jumped. "Yes, Mitch?" I asked, looking up into his face. It had a strained look, and I couldn't imagine what was bothering him.

"I was thinking—," he broke off, and then before I could even blink, his lips had swooped down and were pressed against mine. They were warm, and kind of moist.

For a second I was too stunned to think, and then I realized I was being kissed for the very first time. Before I could decide if I liked it or not Mitch had jumped about a foot away from me.

"I—I thought we'd better get in a little practice in case we want Ty to see us kissing some time," he stammered.

I hadn't been thinking of Ty at all then, but what Mitch said made sense, and it was kind of a relief to know that's what he'd had in mind. If he'd really meant that kiss—well, I didn't want to think about it.

A minute later I let myself in the house. Mom and Dad were in the living room, watching TV. I stuck my head in the door. "You can go to bed now. Your daughter is safely home." That's what Bonnie used to say, but they laughed now, which they hadn't always done when she said it.

"Of course you're safe," Dad said. "You were out with Mitch, weren't you?"

Someday they wouldn't be so smug.

Monday, Gerri called the first committee meeting. We gathered in the small conference room, and it was agreed that I'd welcome the next transfer student who came to Bayside.

Two days later a call came from the registration office. When I reported there I found a sullen-faced girl named Shelley Blake. She hardly said a word as I showed her around the school and campus and chattered about the activities that were open to everyone. At noon I took her to the cafeteria and introduced her to Nancy Dolan, who'd surprised me by being receptive to the idea of making the transfers feel welcome. She'd said she hadn't realized till Carol's article came out how hard it was for them.

"Do you play soccer?" she asked Shelley.

"A little bit." Shelley had begun to brighten, and I had a really good feeling when I went to sit with Mitch.

I told him about Shelley, and he looked over to where she was sitting, talking to Nancy as if they were old friends.

"Good work, Dreyer," he said. His grin of approval made me feel better than ever.

Later I wanted to tell Ty how well the program was working, but I had a feeling he wouldn't be awfully interested. Instead, I moved my head around, hoping he'd notice the different shades the perm had somehow put in my hair, and I said the one thing I was sure would bring a smile to his face.

"Hi, Mr. Quarterback!"

He gave a low, deep laugh that was like music to my ears. "After the big game is out of the way, maybe we can have a Coke together to celebrate," he said.

I nearly choked as I realized I practically had a date with him. "That—that would be fun," was all I could get out.

By the time Kim and I found our seats on the big game day I was too excited to sit down. "Isn't it wonderful to see the stands crowded?" I said, looking around Bayside Stadium. "And isn't it great that the rain went away after the way we were dumped on yesterday?" Football could be played in any kind of weather, of course, but passing is Ty's strong point, and a slippery field would make it harder for him to maneuver into position to fire a long pass.

"There are still some clouds in the sky," Kim observed, looking up.

I glanced up, too. "Those aren't rain clouds," I said. "Anyway, the sun will soon chase them away."

There was some scattered applause now as the visiting team came out. But a minute later it was like an explosion as the Cougars took the field. I joined in the cries of "Go, Cougars, go!" until Kim pulled me down into my seat.

"You won't have any voice left if you keep yelling like that," she told me.

The Eagles got the ball first and managed to score a field goal on our defensive team. Kim groaned like a lot of people in the stands, but I told her not to take it so hard.

"Three points won't do them much good after Ty gets his hands on the ball."

Everyone seemed to agree with me because the cheers were for Ty now, as our offensive team went into action. "We want a touchdown! Come on, Rogers!"

While Ty was huddling with the other players I leaned forward so I could see the bench. Mitch had suited up in case he should be needed, but I knew he wouldn't be . . . not unless Ty got the Cougars so far ahead that Coach Neff benched him for a few minutes so that Mitch could get in a few minutes' playing time after all his hours of practicing.

Ty came out of the huddle to fall back and throw a twenty-yard pass. All the Cougar fans, including me, went crazy. This was just the way we'd expected the game to go. After two more plays Ty quickly handed off the ball to a running back to avoid being sacked. Amid loud cheering, the running back took it the rest of the way for the touchdown. With the conversion we were ahead 7–3.

The Eagles went scoreless during their next possession, then Ty strapped on his helmet and trotted onto the field again.

"What do you want to bet he comes right back with a touchdown pass?" I asked Kim.

She didn't answer. When I looked at her I saw her face was turned up to the sky. I looked up, too, and was surprised to see that a lot of dark clouds had moved in.

"Oh, no, it can't rain!" I wailed. But even as I spoke the words the first drops fell.

What happened after that can best be described as a tragedy. It was pouring by the time Ty came out of the huddle and raised his arm to throw the ball. The defensive players charged him, and when he tried to evade them with his fancy footwork he slipped. To avoid a sack he dumped the ball, and the Eagles were all over it. Within seconds they'd carried it into the end zone. On their next possession they scored again. They were ahead 17–7.

No matter how hard he tried, Ty couldn't get anything going. I heard the people around me begin to grumble that he should give up his passing game and start handing the ball off to his running backs more.

I felt sick, hearing Ty criticized. "They were all cheering him a minute ago," I complained to Kim. "It's not his fault it began to rain."

She studied her fingernails, something she did when she didn't want to comment on something.

"Don't worry," I said, more to myself than

to her. "Ty will come back in the second half."

I felt a little better then and even managed to enjoy the half-time show. Randy was playing with the band, and I joined Kim in applauding as they marched around the soppy field. All the time, though, I was thinking, *If only it would stop raining. If only the sun would come out and dry the grass.*

Then I found out it would be too late for Ty even if that happened. Just before the Cougars came out for the second half, an announcement came over the loudspeaker. "Mitch Conley is now playing quarterback for the Bayside Cougers."

There were cries of dismay. That meant that Coach Neff had given up hope of winning the game and just wanted to save Ty any more humiliation. Since nothing was expected of Mitch, losing wouldn't be as hard on him as it would be on Ty.

I watched Mitch in the huddle, snapping out signals. I wondered if the team had enough confidence in him to even follow his game plan. Some people were already leaving the stands.

I guess maybe they sat down again after Mitch's first play. I wasn't sure because I was on my feet screaming as Mitch put the ball in motion. It was only a short pass, but the receiver ran it for a first down. The

Eagles had charged Mitch, but dancing around in the pocket wasn't his style of play. He stood where he was like he was rooted to the spot till he'd found an open man, then he took the sack.

Pretty soon there were cries of "Conley, Conley!" I joined in, thrilled for my old friend, although my heart was broken for Ty. He hadn't come out for the second half, which meant something must be wrong. Most players sat on the bench to cheer on their teammates even though they were out of the game.

"I bet Ty is hurt," I told Kim during a time-out.

"I doubt it," she said.

"Then why hasn't he come out to at least root for the team?"

She shrugged. "I wouldn't know."

I knew she had some opinion on it because she had an opinion on everything, but I'd learned not to press her where Ty was concerned. Most of the time I didn't like what she said about him. She probably thought he was being a poor sport.

Mitch kept moving the ball a few yards at a time, mixing up his short passes with running plays. His game wasn't flashy like Ty's, but pretty soon the Cougars had caught up with the Eagles. The game was tied!

It was still tied, with only two minutes to

play. Everyone was on their feet, screaming, "We want a touchdown! Go, Conley, go!" Even Kim was excited, and we jumped up and down together, yelling, "Come on, Mitch!"

As Mitch went into a huddle with only twenty seconds to play, he held up his hand, asking the crowd to quiet down so the team could hear him call the signals. It was an authoritative gesture that the fans responded to at once, and my heart swelled with pride. I'd never dreamed that my quiet, rather shy friend was such a leader.

When the huddle broke up, Mitch fell back and quickly passed the ball off to Gordie Holmes. Gordie moved to the left, and the crowd groaned as he ran into a solid wall of Eagle defenders.

A second later there was a gasp as the fans realized Mitch hadn't passed the ball at all. Holding it close to his body, he'd run to the right, and with all the Eagles guarding Gordie, he'd carried the ball across the goal line. Everyone went wild.

"What happened?" Kim asked, bewildered.

I could hardly answer for laughing and cheering. "Mitch pulled a quarterback sneak!"

She got it then, and we both became practically hysterical, cheering Mitch and the whole team. We'd won the game!

* * *

Kim had agreed to meet Randy at The Last
Straw after the game, and I was glad to tag
along. I was so excited, yet I felt so mixed
up, too, that I couldn't bear to go home just
yet. I was thrilled for Mitch, but still, I was
unhappy for Ty, and worried, besides. No
matter what Kim said, I was afraid he'd
been hurt.

The Last Straw was a madhouse. Everyone was there, celebrating Bayside's victory.
There was even a cheer for me when I went
in because I was supposed to be Mitch's girl.
Somebody I didn't know saw that Kim and I
got a booth. And somebody else brought us
Cokes.

"Is Mitch coming in later?" I was asked. I
had to say I didn't know. My thoughts
before the game had been of Ty, and I hadn't
thought to ask Mitch his plans.

"How does it feel to be a hero's girl?" Kim
asked me.

She was acting as if she didn't know the
truth about Mitch and me, and before I
could tell her to get real, Randy joined us.
Kim greeted him with a kiss, and I thought
how lucky she was not to be leading a
double life like I was.

A few minutes later a cheer went up, and I
didn't even have to look toward the door to
know Mitch had come in. I moved over on
the bench, and grinning shyly, he slid in

beside me. I mimicked Kim, and gave him a kiss, only I planted mine on his jaw and not his lips. His grin widened. And then he stared as somebody set a Coke and a huge dish of fries in front of him.

"What's this for?" he asked the boy.

"Just call it the spoils of victory."

"I didn't expect anything like this," Mitch said in amazement when the boy had left.

"You deserve some spoils," I told him. "All that extra practice really paid off. You're the hero of the game." *And poor Ty loses out*, I couldn't help thinking.

Randy leaned across the table and whacked Mitch on the shoulder. "You were great, man! I hope Coach Neff doesn't forget it when he picks his team next year."

Suddenly the place became quiet. You could hear the dishes rattling in the kitchen. I looked toward the door and saw Ty standing there, holding his right arm as if he were in pain. For once Gloria was not with him.

Mitch saw Ty, too, and called out, "Rogers! Why don't you sit here with us?"

Ty smiled faintly as he approached the booth. "Thanks." He sat down gingerly, as if the slightest movement hurt him a lot.

"You got a bad flipper?" Randy asked, not sounding a bit sympathetic.

"I hurt my wrist in the first couple of minutes of play," Ty said. "I wanted to drop in here for a minute, but then I'll see the family doctor. I wouldn't be surprised if something is broken."

"What did the trainer say?" Randy asked. "If it's that bad, you'd think he would have at least bandaged it."

"I didn't want him to touch it," Ty replied stiffly. "I'm sure my parents will want me to see a specialist in sports injuries."

A minute later when he went to the counter, Randy said, "He'd do better to see a specialist in sportsmanship. He's just trying to rob Mitch of his glory, pretending he would have won the game if he hadn't been hurt."

"Oh, I don't know about that," Mitch argued quietly. "Playing conditions were pretty bad out there, especially for Ty's kind of game."

"For his showboating, you mean."

I'd always liked Randy, but if I'd spoken to him right then I think I would have bit his head off. He just didn't understand Ty, and he had no right to judge him.

Ty came back with a cup of coffee, which .he held awkwardly in his left hand. Imagine Ty doing anything awkwardly! It was really heartbreaking. He was probably drinking coffee, I thought, because he hoped it would give him some energy and make him forget how lousy he felt.

In a few minutes his brother Hank came

over to the booth. He'd been hanging out with some seniors on the other side of the room. "I'm going home now," he told Ty. "You want a lift?"

He didn't sound very concerned about his brother's injury. He was tall and had the same coloring as Ty, but he wasn't nearly as good-looking. I decided there was probably some sibling rivalry there. Kim had explained sibling rivalry to me a long time ago, when she'd told me she was glad she was an only child.

Ty rose slowly, and at least I could see the suffering in his face. He was gallant, though. Just before he moved away he said, "Oh, congratulations, Conley. With me getting hurt like this, I'm sure glad you were able to save the game for me."

"Thanks, Ty. See ya later," Mitch called out as he dug into the french fries. "Hey, you guys, help me out," he said a minute later. "I won't eat any dinner if I go through all these."

We all took a couple of fries to please him, then I said I'd better call Dad, who'd agreed to pick Kim and me up whenever we were ready to go home. We were all soaked, so everyone was willing to break it up.

When Dad pulled up to the curb, I motioned Mitch to get in the front with him while Kim and I sat in the back. Randy took off with a guy who lived in the same part of town he did.

"Nice going, my boy!" Dad said, shaking hands with Mitch. "I heard the results of the game on the radio. You really came through like a champion."

"Thanks, Mr. Dreyer." Mitch gave a pleased grin.

"I wish you could have seen the quarterback sneak he pulled," I said. "It was beautiful!"

"A quarterback sneak, huh? That's a mighty clever play when it works," Dad remarked.

"Mitch made it work!" I declared. "He—" Suddenly I broke off as I realized I was praising Mitch to the skies, and not giving a thought to poor Ty, who must feel terrible. And maybe his wrist was broken, too. . . .

When we got home Kim ran across the street, and Mitch headed for his house. "You must be proud of your boyfriend," Daddy told me.

"I am," I said. But I wasn't sure if I meant Mitch, who was so modest in victory, or Ty, who was suffering the agony of defeat.

Chapter 9

Monday morning Ty showed up at school with his right wrist bandaged. He stood on the front steps with Gloria and some other kids around him. I could see he was explaining how the injury to his wrist had happened.

I'd walked to school with Mitch, but some boys had stopped him to congratulate him on the game, and I walked up the stairs alone. When I reached Ty, I stopped.

"I see your doctor did find something wrong with your wrist," I said, my voice full of sympathy.

"Yeah." He shook off Gloria's hand, and stepped away from the group. Touching my shoulder he said, "I'm sorry I didn't get that touchdown for you, Denise. But you know what happened." He let go of my shoulder to hold his right wrist.

"Don't even think about it," I said "I'm just sorry you got hurt." I couldn't help adding, "It sure was lucky, though, that Mitch came through the way he did."

The way his face darkened, I knew I'd said the wrong thing. He didn't want to talk about Mitch. He wanted sympathy—the way we all do when we're hurting.

I made amends the best I could. "I hope your wrist heals quickly." That brought a smile to his face.

"Thanks. Hey, let's have a Coke together real soon. You know we talked about it. We can go to The Straw."

I thought he'd forgotten about it, or that he hadn't really meant the invitation. He seemed really eager, though, and my heart did all kinds of acrobatics. He was really interested in me! Still, I was supposedly serious about Mitch, so I couldn't make a date right away. Maybe Mitch and I could start to cool it a little. Then when Ty asked me again I could jump at the invitation.

"I'll have to see," I answered carefully.

"I understand." He knew what was on my mind and gave me such a deep glance I felt as if I were drowning in it.

That afternoon Kim came home with me. Mom had decided to rough out her column at the *Courier* office so we had the house to ourselves. Since I knew I'd have time to clean up the kitchen before Mom got home, we didn't worry so much about making a mess. We made grilled-cheese sandwiches and chocolate shakes, garnishing the shakes with whipped cream, and the sandwiches with pickles and various relishes. While we ate at the breakfast bar I told Kim the wonderful news I'd been saving for the right moment.

"Ty asked me out again today." I filled her in on what he'd said about us having a Coke at The Straw. "What do you think now about my chances of going to the Christmas Ball with him?"

"I guess they're pretty good," she conceded, but she didn't sound very enthusiastic. She had something on her mind, and knowing her as well as I did, I could be sure she wouldn't keep it to herself for long. After she'd taken another bite of her sandwich and stirred the shake with her straw, she finally spoke. "You know what this is all about, don't you, Denny? Since Mitch is a school hero now, your being his girl is really important to Ty. Taking you away from Mitch would be a feather in his cap."

"He mentioned the Coke date before he even knew Mitch was going to win the game!" My voice quivered with indignation.

"But he didn't follow up on it. And he didn't say anything about The Straw."

"He would have!"

"Maybe," she said.

I got up and started to straighten the

kitchen. I'd hardly ever been so angry with Kim. Even when she changed the subject, asking me when we expected Bonnie home for Thanksgiving, I just said, "On Wednesday," and kept on putting stuff back in the fridge. Finally she said she'd better go—she had some studying to do, and I said, "Yeah, me, too."

Later I thought over our conversation and decided she was probably right, in a way. Ty had shown more interest in me today than he ever had before, and probably it was because he thought I was Mitch's girl, and Mitch was sort of a hero now. But that wasn't so terrible. I'd known all the time he was only interested in girls who dated, and it followed that the more important the boy they went with, the more attracted he'd be to them. It was like going after a trophy. And going after a trophy was a natural challenge to him.

When I came home from school Wednesday, Bonnie was in the kitchen having a cup of tea with Mom. I was really glad to see her, and we gave each other a big hug. Then Mom said if we'd excuse her she'd like to get on with her preparations for Thanksgiving dinner.

"I'm trying a new kind of dressing, and I need to concentrate, so you girls go someplace, will you?"

Good old Mom. She really came through

at times. She knew Bonnie and I were dying to be alone so we could have a real sister-to-sister talk. We went up to Bonnie's room. Being neat like Mom, she'd already put away her clothes and suitcases. There was a framed picture of a serious-looking young man on her dresser.

"That's Griff," she told me. "Isn't he a doll?"

He wasn't my type, but I said he sure was, then we sat on the matching slipper chairs Mom and Dad had given Bonnie on her sixteenth birthday. Bonnie told me Griff was going to be a teacher.

"I'm thinking of changing my major, too. Teaching is so important, and Griff says that's finally being recognized. He thinks that in a few years good teachers will be rewarded like engineers and management people are now."

Love sure changed your life, I thought. Bonnie had gone away to college with the idea of becoming a computer specialist. She'd never heard of a Griff, or given a thought to teaching. While this was going through my mind, she said she was glad I was going with Mitch.

"I think you two being in love is just beautiful . . . you and the boy next door—well, almost next door. It's a real love story. And I see you got yourself all prettied up for him."

Mitch didn't care what I looked like, I

thought, but I only said that Kim had given me a perm. I wondered if Bonnie had always been so pretty, and I just hadn't noticed, or if being in love had made her eyes so bright and given her skin such a lovely glow. She had hazel eyes like I did, and the same brown hair, but she looked beautiful without even trying.

We talked till Mom called us downstairs to help get dinner on. We were just having a light supper because Mom wanted everybody to save their appetite for the next day. I was glad when Mom said we were going to have a traditional Thanksgiving dinner. She promised that the only new recipe would be the dressing, and even that only had a few extra herbs in it. There are times to experiment, I thought, but there are other times when you want things to be the way they've always been.

The next day Aunt June and Uncle Art came up from San Jose with their two kids, Jennifer, who was thirteen, and Jimmy, who was eleven. While I didn't see my cousins often, I still had a feeling of family with them, and it was nice for us all to have Thanksgiving dinner together.

At the table, everyone took turns saying what they were thankful for. Jimmy, who had kind of a smart mouth, eyed the turkey and said he was glad he had a good appetite. Jennifer was glad she had her braces off. Aunt June, who was the emotional type, got choked up and couldn't say anything, so Uncle Art spoke for them both, saying they were grateful to be included in our Thanksgiving celebration.

Mom was grateful we were all in good health, and Dad as usual, said he was thankful we were all together. Bonnie echoed his words. When it was my turn I mumbled something about being happy for all my blessings while I wondered if Ty and I would ever spend a Thanksgiving together.

Sunday morning Bonnie got in her vintage Mustang and headed back to San Francisco. Kim and her parents had gone to Marin County to spend the holiday weekend in a cabin they owned there. With Bonnie gone, and Kim away, I got so lonely that shortly after lunch I got on my bike and pedaled down to Mitch's.

Susie was out front. "Want to shoot baskets?" she asked.

"Not right now. Is Mitch home?"

"Yeah." She sounded disgusted, but then she turned philosophical. "I guess some day you won't want to shoot baskets anymore at all. Girls get so silly when they fall in love." She opened her mouth and bellowed, "Mitch! Denny wants you!"

If anyone could bring back the town crier it would be Susie.

Mitch came out the door. "Don't you know it's raining?" he asked me.

"It's barely drizzling . . . you made of sugar?"

He swung on his bike. "Where're we going?"

"I don't know. I just feel like taking a ride."

We pedaled along, and without even deciding where we were going we took the road to Deer Creek. It was a woodsy area, and even when it rained hard you could always find a dry spot under the trees.

With the recent rain the creek was high. We found a couple of flat rocks on the bank, and with our ski jackets and jeans, and the trees almost meeting above us, we were pretty comfortable.

"Remember when we got the bright idea there might be gold in that thar creek?" Mitch chuckled.

I gave him a shove that nearly pushed him off his rock. "That was *your* bright idea, mister! I just went along for the ride."

"Okay, okay, I've gone along on a few wild-goose chases with you," he reminded me.

I had had some pretty far-out ideas in my time so I didn't dare say any more.

"You know, it seems like your welcoming committee is doing some good work," Mitch said after a while. "One of the new guys has volunteered to paint posters for the Christmas dance, and I hear he's real talented."

"That's Carol's doing," I said. "Even when I learned from Marie how rough the transfers had it, nothing would have happened if Carol hadn't written that article."

Mitch grinned at me. "You're modest, too."

"So are you."

He knew what I was talking about and pretty soon he said, "How's it going with Ty?"

"He mentioned us going to The Straw."

I thought that might bring another grin to Mitch's face, because it meant we might soon get to act like friends at school, instead of a dating couple. He didn't grin, though, and a minute later he said we'd better go.

"It's too wet to be sitting here."

Back on our own street I offered to make hot chocolate, but he said his dad was making some shelves in his workshop, and he should be helping.

"I'll put marshmallows in it," I coaxed.

"Thanks, anyway. I'll see you."

Gosh, boys could be hard to understand even when you thought you knew them as well as you knew yourself.

Monday I was glad to go back to school. And by now, with the big game and Thanksgiving behind us, there was a new excitement in the air. Everyone was beginning to look forward to the Christmas dance, and excitement was rising as the selection of a sweetheart couple drew nearer. We all figured that Linda Smith and Joel Pierce had the selection all sewn up. Although they'd had a few fights they always patched them up. And other than that, they seemed the perfect pair. I thought they were a wonderful choice, and I was pulling for them.

Mostly, though, I was pulling for Ty to ask me to go to the ball with him. I couldn't help thinking my chances were good, especially since he seemed to be losing interest in Gloria. More and more I saw him alone in the halls, or walking along with other guys. Gloria didn't seem to care very much, either. One afternoon she drove off with a junior named Kirk who drove a cute little Fiat.

At first I was excited because they seemed to have broken up, but in the end it didn't seem to do me any good because Ty began to look around at other girls. So now I had more complications than ever. I finally decided to put on some pressure. One day I waited until he was in the cafeteria line, and then I hurried to fall in behind him. I sort of crowded him, and he turned around.

"Oh, hi," he said. Football was over for the year, and Mitch's fame had sort of died away. I couldn't count on being his girl friend to get Ty to take me to the dance.

"How's your wrist coming along?" I asked him, striking the one note I knew would get his attention.

He didn't wear a bandage anymore, but

still when he touched his wrist with his other hand he winced. "The doctor says it's doing as well as can be expected." He drew a sigh. "I just hope nothing goes wrong. My dad was All-American, and his heart is set on me following in his footsteps. Hank's sure no athlete," he added in a tone that confirmed my theory of sibling rivalry.

"I'm sure you'll make All-American," I told him. "Gee, the year is just zipping by, isn't it? Before we know it, it'll be Christmas." He gave me his puzzled look, and I rushed on to make my point—as boldly as I dared. "That means the Christmas Ball is coming up soon. Do you think you'll go?"

"Probably. I haven't made up my mind yet." He was looking over my shoulder at someone who'd moved in behind me. I could smell her perfume.

"I'll probably go, too," I said, "although I haven't a thing to wear." I laughed, and gave a meaningless wave of my hand, trying to be so animated he'd stop looking over my shoulder and concentrate on me.

He did, for a minute, but then his bewildered look was back, as if he wondered why he was standing there talking to me. "The line seems to be moving," he said at last, and grabbed a tray.

I glanced over my shoulder. The girl behind me was Marie. Oh, great! If she and Ty got together I'd have no one but myself to blame. Before Carol had written the article

I'd inspired, Ty wouldn't have looked at a transfer, and Marie would have frozen him out if he had.

"Hi, Denny," Marie said. "I heard you talking about the Christmas dance. I guess that's a tradition at Bayside, huh?"

"Yeah, it sure is. I hope you get to go," I managed to say. I knew she'd only go with a superior boy like Ty.

"I don't usually go to such things, but I'll see," she replied.

We both smiled, and I turned toward the counter. She'll go if Ty asks her, I thought.

The next day Gerri Carson again called me out of study hall. I assumed it had something to do with the welcoming committee, but instead of leading the way to the small conference room we went down the hall to Mrs. McGrew's office. She was the vice-principal and student advisor. I was surprised to see Mitch in her office, as well as some of the student officers. I couldn't imagine what was up. Had Mitch and I gotten in some kind of trouble without knowing it? Maybe we'd been acting too affectionate, holding hands, and him putting his arm around my waist sometimes as we walked along the halls. I looked at Mitch, who motioned me to sit on a chair beside him. I could see he was as bewildered as I was.

"Now, then," Mrs. McGrew said, looking

around the room, "I think it's time to tell Denise and Mitch what this is all about."

She was a plumpish woman with graying hair—sort of motherly-looking, although she had a reputation for being a stern disciplinarian. She smiled and I could tell that she hadn't brought Mitch and me here to give us a bad time. I began to relax, and I could feel Mitch relax, too, in the chair beside me.

"Denise and Mitch," Mrs. McGrew said, "I'm sure you'll be delighted to learn you've been chosen as sweethearts of the Christmas Ball."

"What!" Mitch gasped.

I was speechless. In fact, I doubted if I'd ever be able to speak again.

Light laughter rippled around the room. Mrs. McGrew laughed, too.

"I know you must be very surprised. Usually the nominating committee chooses upperclassmen for the honor, but this year they decided to make an exception." Her smile widened, and I tried to smile back but I was still in shock.

"We feel that you are the perfect couple to preside over the dance," she continued. "Your attitude toward each other is exceptional at your age. It clearly springs from a warm friendship based on mutual respect and interests, as well as affection. We feel you typify the goodwill and loving spirit of the season."

She went on to say that we qualified in other ways, too, citing my work with the welcoming committee that showed a desire to help others, and to serve Bayside. Mitch had distinguished himself on the football field, bringing the regional championship to Bayside.

"But Mrs. McGrew—," I finally got out. I had to tell her the truth, that Mitch and I weren't sweethearts at all—that we'd just been pretending. . . .

Before I could say another word Mitch caught my hand and squeezed it so hard I almost yelled.

"I'm sure I speak for Denise in saying we both thank you and the committee for this honor, Mrs. McGrew," he said. "We'll do our best to prove worthy of it."

"That's settled, then." Mrs. McGrew stood up, ending the meeting. She only added that the dance committee would now go ahead with the publicity, including the announcement of our selection as sweethearts of the Ball.

Mitch took my arm and pulled me out into the hall. I couldn't move on my own power. Had any scheme in the history of the world ever backfired like this? Sweethearts of the ball—Mitch and me! It was an impossible situation, and we simply couldn't go through with it.

Chapter 10

"We have to tell Mrs. McGrew the truth," I said when Mitch and I finally got a chance to talk. We'd both had to hurry back to class when we'd left the vice-principal's office, and all the rest of the day we hadn't had a minute alone. Even after school Mom had picked me up for a dental appointment, so I didn't get a chance to see him at all. The minute I got home from the dentist I dashed down the street.

Mitch was waiting for me. We went to the garage and sat in his mother's car, one of our favorite places when we wanted to have a serious talk. As bad a jam as we were in right now I could tell that Mitch liked the feeling of sitting behind the wheel.

"We simply can't go through with it," I said more urgently, as he just sat there, probably pretending to himself he was driving. "We'd be frauds. What qualifies us to be sweethearts of the ball—collecting trash together? Shooting baskets? Dumping on each other whenever something bothers us? That doesn't make us sweethearts, it makes us friends. Sure, they want a couple who have a friendly relationship, but there's also supposed to be a big romance between them. Why did you say we'd do our best to be worthy of the honor when you know very well we're not worthy of it?"

Mitch looked at me finally, and I could see now he hadn't been pretending he was driving. He'd been thinking very seriously about the situation we were in.

"We have to go through with it, Denny," he said. His voice was getting deep, I noticed—as if that had anything to do with anything.

"Why, I'd like to know!" I responded. "We can go to Mrs. McGrew tomorrow and tell her we've changed our minds. We can tell her we've broken up!"

Mitch shook his head in the stubborn way he had when he was very sure he was right about something. "We're not going to do that. We got ourselves into this, and we're going to see it through. The committee is already going ahead with their publicity. We can't let them down."

I refused to accept that. "When we started pretending we were sweethearts there was no way we could imagine anything like this was going to happen."

"That's true, but it has happened. We've been weaving a tangled web with our deception," Mitch said quietly. "Just like that quotation . . . you know the one."

"Yeah, I know," I mumbled.

At that point Susie came through the adjoining kitchen door. "What are you doing in Mama's car?" she demanded of Mitch in her brattiest tone. "Are you going to drive it? If you do I'm coming along."

"You know I've sat here lots of times before," Mitch told her.

"But you're almost old enough to drive now."

"Almost doesn't count. So do me a favor, will you, and go play with your dolls?"

"You know I don't play with dolls!" She couldn't have been more indignant if she'd been accused of stealing. Before she disappeared into the kitchen she remembered her manners enough to say, "Hi, Denny."

It occurred to me that if Mitch and I did have a romance going, she'd be a serious impediment to it.

Mitch turned to me again. "How about it, Denise? Will you pretend we're really sweethearts for just that one night?"

His eyes looked anxiously into mine. I was surprised that he felt so strongly about us being the sweethearts. It wasn't the kind of thing I thought he'd go in for, but it obvi-

ously meant a lot to him. All of a sudden I
made up my mind.

"Why not?" I said, putting a bright note in
my voice. "I guess it's the least we can do for
dear old Bayside High."

I don't know who hugged whom first, but
we just about choked each other as we
agreed we'd put on such a good show no one
would ever guess that the sweethearts of the
Christmas Ball were just good friends.

As soon as I left Mitch's, I ran over to Kim's.
Luckily she was home. I would have put out
an A.P.B. for her if she hadn't been. She let
me in and hurried me up to her room. Her
mother was in the living room with some of
the cast of *The Glass Menagerie.* Kim
whispered that she was laying low so she
wouldn't be pressed into reading a part as
she sometimes was.

In the comparative safety of her room, we
flopped on the bed, me at the foot, she at the
head, in the lotus position. I'd tried that
once, and it had taken both Kim and her
mother to get me out of it, so I just drew my
knees up to my chin.

"I called you a while ago to see if I could
come over, but the answering machine was
on," Kim told me.

"Oh, yeah. I was at Mitch's."

"It seems to me you're seeing a lot of Mitch
lately. Is it getting serious? I've noticed you
don't talk about Ty as much as you used to."

I threw a pillow at her. "Just because I don't talk about him every minute doesn't mean I don't think about him all the time."

She threw the pillow back at me. "So, okay, what's up? Even if I didn't know you so well I'd know you were bursting with some news."

"You're right," I admitted. "The most incredible thing has happened."

"Like what?"

"Like Mitch and I have been chosen sweethearts of the Christmas Ball."

I'd handed her some big surprises lately, but nothing like this. When she'd stopped sputtering and had begun to speak coherently she began to bombard me with questions, and finally I spilled out the whole story, right down to Mitch convincing me we had to go through with it.

"There was something I couldn't tell him, though. Oh, I guess I could have, but for some reason I didn't. This means I won't be able to go to the dance with Ty, even if he asks me. And I swore I would go with him."

Kim stared at me. "I can't believe you see that as a problem. In the first place Ty hasn't asked you to the dance, and you don't know that he would. The important thing, though, is that this is the best way in the world to impress him. Do you remember how beautiful Christine Thomas looked last year, as sweetheart of the ball?"

I remembered, all right. With the spotlight on her, and in her long white, full-skirted dress with rows and rows of little tucks, and a corsage of red baby roses, she'd looked like a fairy-tale princess. Before that I'd always thought she was quite ordinary-looking.

"Yeah, I see your point," I told Kim. "There's something magic about being sweetheart of the ball."

Kim nodded vigorously. "It's pure magic. Every boy there will fall in love with you, and every girl will fall in love with Mitch."

My mouth fell open at that. But then I realized that I had a brief crush on Christine's partner last year. He'd looked so different from the skinny kid I saw around school every day. Would Mitch suddenly look like Prince Charming?

Kim was rushing on. "Your mother will have to let you buy the most fabulous dress in the county." She half-closed her eyes. "You'll wear silver slippers, I think—with high heels, of course. And you'll have to have your hair done. Mom swears by Mr. Anthony. Mitch will send you a corsage—"

"How do you know he will?"

"Because that's the right thing for the boy to do, and Mitch always does the right thing, doesn't he?"

"I . . . guess so."

"You know he does!" She suddenly flopped forward and gave me a hug. "Oh, Denny, this is the most wonderful thing that's ever happened!"

I hugged her back. "It is pretty great, isn't it?"

We talked some more, and I really began to get excited. "You'll help me look for a dress, and shoes, and everything else I'll need, won't you?"

"Of course I will. I can hardly wait. Someday I may make a career of helping people shop."

I knew it was selfish of me, but right now I was too involved in my own affairs to even tell Kim I thought that was a great idea. "And you'll teach me to dance, won't you? Remember last year the sweethearts opened the dance by doing a waltz. You know how to waltz, don't you?"

"I should after all the years Mom made me take dancing lessons. When she decided I'd never be a ballerina she had me take ballroom, on the grounds that that was at least a social asset."

Finally I asked Kim why she thought Linda and Joel hadn't been chosen when everyone had been so sure they would be. "Carol has a good nose for those things, and she was sure they'd be sweethearts of the ball this year."

"You may remember I pointed out that they fight a lot, and that it seems to be a power struggle between them. What if they had a falling out just before the dance?"

"I bet that was it," I agreed. "The committee was probably afraid to take a chance."

I went home then. Even though Mom was in the den with the door closed, and I knew I wasn't supposed to bother her, I tapped on the door anyway. I felt I had to tell her my news. It was the most exciting thing that had ever happened to me.

"Mom!" I said.

There was a long silence, and I was afraid that when it was broken it would be because the roof had blown off. Nobody ever bothered Mom when she was writing the first draft of her column.

"What is it, Denise?" she said at last, in a fairly calm voice.

"I—have some news."

I could hear her chair scraping back. "Come in," she said. There was a terrible calmness in her tone now as if she were prepared to hear something shattering. When I opened the door she was standing in the middle of the room, looking so vulnerable I was glad my news was nothing that would hurt her.

"I hope it was all right to bother you, Mom. Like I told you, I have some news. Mitch and I have been chosen sweethearts of the Christmas dance."

It took her a second to register what I'd said, then she rushed forward and hugged me. "That's wonderful, Denny! I'm so proud of you, and Dad will be, too."

I was doing a lot of hugging today, I thought, as I put my arms around her and squeezed.

"Why don't we have a cup of tea while we talk this over?" Mom surprised me by saying. It was the first time she'd ever invited me to have tea with her. Bonnie had been sixteen before she'd asked her.

When I tasted the tea I didn't like it much, but because I realized it was a rite of passage to adulthood I enjoyed it a lot. Mom wanted to know everything that had happened that day, and I told her about Mitch and me being called to Mrs. McGrew's office, and every word that had been said there.

That night at dinner Mom repeated the whole story to Dad. Smiling proudly at me he said, "I told you you'd be the belle of the ball before long."

I felt more like a fraud than ever, but I managed to grin. "You sure called it."

After that everything moved fast. Mitch and I had to pose for publicity pictures, and posters began to go up all over school. There was a rehearsal in the gym where I came down from the stage to meet Mitch who was waiting for me at the foot of the stairs. Then we pretended to waltz down the middle of the room. There was no music, so we didn't really dance. We just took hands and whirled around, but everybody applauded. I wondered if that would happen the night of the ball.

Mitch and I stuck closer together than ever now, and we received congratulations from all over. One day Ty spoke to me when I went into history. He was standing by his desk.

"I see you're going to be sweetheart of the Christmas dance," he said.

I'd dressed in such a hurry that morning I hadn't put on any makeup except a dash of lip gloss. My hair was beginning to look raggedy, and I'd worn jeans and an old sweater because it was raining. No wonder Ty looked at me as if he wondered why I'd been chosen for such an honor.

"Yes," I said. With him looking at me that way, I didn't try to prolong the conversation. "I guess I'd better get to my seat," I muttered. That day when we'd laughed together about Mrs. Cole's sarcastic remarks seemed a long time ago.

I thought of something else as I slunk into my seat. He'd never followed up on the invitation for me to have a Coke with him at The Last Straw. My being a hero's girl hadn't impressed him for long . . . not after the worship of the football hero died away, and a basketball star was now the toast of the school.

But the next day I found out that Ty had a different reason for losing what little interest he'd had in me. He and Marie walked into the cafeteria together. She smiled and waved at me, having no reason to suspect, of course, that she had taken away my great love.

I talked it over with Kim on the bus that afternoon. "I like Marie," I said. "I think she's a nice girl, but she's not right for Ty. To begin with, she probably won't be here for long, and besides, she's as self-absorbed in her way as Gloria. She's not vain about her looks, but she knows what she wants, and I don't think she's the type to compromise."

"You mean Ty needs someone who'll cater to him."

"I don't mean that at all!" I protested. "He just needs someone who—" I couldn't explain exactly what I meant, so I gave up and said, "All that's happened is that I'm back where I started with him. He's still looking for the right girl, and someday he'll see she's been there all the time."

When I spoke to Mom about shopping for my dress she said, "When would you like us to go, dear?"

Us? As calmly as I could I said that Kim had offered to help me look for my dress and the other things I'd need.

"Kim has some very extravagant ideas," Mom said. "I think it would be better if I went along, too."

"I won't spend too much, Mom," I promised frantically. "You set the limit and I won't go a penny over it."

"I don't want you to buy anything too grown up."

"I *am* grown up, Mom."

"Of course you are, Denny. I mean I don't want you to buy anything too sophisticated."

"I won't." I was willing to promise anything. Mom *couldn't* pick out my dress. I could just see myself in something juvenile, with ruffles and a Peter Pan collar.

"Well, all right, I'll trust you and Kim to find something suitable," she finally said. "You can always exchange it, if necessary."

"Sure I can," I said eagerly. Once I found my dream dress, though, I knew I'd die rather than to give it up.

On Saturday Kim and I went to the mall. I guess she was right when she told me about developing shopping muscles because we were there most of the day and I didn't get tired at all. Even if I'd been exhausted, though, I would have revived when I found my dress. At first I was afraid to even try it on, it was so exquisite, so unlike anything I'd ever worn before.

Kim fell in love with it, too. "If you don't buy it, I will," she threatened. But she didn't mean it, and when she took it from the rack she handed it to me. "Let's find a dressing room."

When I slipped the confection of ivory-colored lace and rustling taffeta over my head, and it fell gracefully into place, I stared unbelievingly at myself.

"Is that really me?"

Kim laughed. "Just wait till dance night when you have your slippers and bag, and your hair done up."

"Up?" I echoed.

"Up," she said firmly. "We'll leave everything to Mr. Anthony."

"But upsweeps are so glamorous and I'm not a glamorous person," I objected.

"You will be the night of the ball."

I wondered if she was right. Would the magic of being sweetheart of the ball work for me? Or would Mr. Anthony's fancy hairdo fall down while I was dancing? Would I trip on my high heels as I walked down from the stage to meet Mitch? I could just picture everybody howling with laughter.

But, oh, please, my guardian angel, don't let that happen! For that one night let me be beautiful and glamorous—the girl of every boy's dreams—especially Ty's.

Chapter 11

There were times during the next week when I thought the day of the dance would never come. It finally did, though, and by then I was so excited I wasn't sure I could handle it. What if I went into some kind of nervous collapse?

Luckily, Kim took charge, so I didn't have to think about anything. She even went with me to Mr. Anthony's on Saturday morning. I think I would have stopped him when he began to pull my hair to the top of my head if she hadn't been there to give me a warning look. And when he was through I was glad she had. I was stunned at how becoming the glamorous style was to me.

"We'll tuck a sprig of holly into your topknot," Kim decided.

When Mitch's corsage was delivered in the

middle of the afternoon, Kim answered the door, and let me have a peek at the florist's arrangement of tiny silver bells nestled against smilax leaves. Then she put it in the fridge so the leaves would stay fresh.

"Please give me another dancing lesson!" I begged a minute later.

"You don't need one. After our lesson last night, you'll do fine," she said, "but—" Resigned, she went to the stereo and put on one of Mom's records: One Hundred of the World's Best-loved Waltzes. It was the opening dance Mitch and I would do to start the ball that I was worried about. After that I could hide in the rest room if I felt I had to.

Later, just before she went home to get herself ready for the dance, Kim drew a gardenia-scented bath for me. It was like having a lady in waiting.

The dance started at nine. "You have to eat something," Mom insisted.

"I couldn't. Please don't ask me to, Mom."

"Sip a little broth or I'm afraid you'll get sick."

"I'm sick already."

"But, honey—"

"Leave the girl alone, Laura," Dad said so gently that Mom couldn't possibly take offense. *I owe him a big hug,* I thought, as I escaped to my room.

Kim had already helped me lay out my things—my new bikini panties and wispy bra, my sheer pantyhose, and my little silver clutch bag. My fingers trembled nervously so that they were almost useless, but when Mom taped on my door and asked if she could help me, I said I was getting along fine.

I managed to get into my underwear and stockings, then I put on my silver slippers with the slender ankle strap, and practiced walking in them. I guess practice does make perfect, because I'd been wearing them for a while every day that week, and at last I no longer felt as if I were on stilts.

The very last thing I did, after carefully applying my makeup, was to slip my dress over my head. That was quite an operation, because I dared not mess up my hair. Besides all of Mr. Anthony's work, Kim had already tucked the sprig of holly into my topknot. She had a knack for doing such things, and if I messed up the holly I'd never be able to get it right.

After I had the dress on I closed my eyes for a minute. When I opened them I stared at the girl in the mirror—the fairy-tale princess who had somehow taken my place. The next second I ran to the door.

"Mom!" I called. "You can come in now."

She came running. And she stared, too. "Oh, Denny—Denise—you're lovely."

"It's the dress that's lovely."

"No, it's you. I'd hug you if I weren't afraid

to crush your corsage." A mist came and went in her eyes, then she said, "Excuse me a minute, I'll be right back."

While she was gone on her secret mission I admired the dress that had turned me into such a vision that I hardly knew myself. The ivory-colored lace gave my skin a warm glow. The full, ankle-length taffeta under-skirt rustled at my every move. The scoop neck showed quite a bit of me, but the little cap sleeves gave it a demure touch that I was pretty sure had kept Mom from finding it too "sophisticated." Translation: too grown up for me.

I turned from the mirror when Mom came back to my room. She was holding something I couldn't see, but then she opened her hand, and I gasped. Nestled in her palm was a single strand of pearls that was a family heirloom and her most precious pos-session. She'd loaned them to Bonnie only once, on her graduation night.

"Oh, Mom!" I cried. "Are you really going to let me wear your pearls?"

"It looks that way, doesn't it?" she said as she clasped them around my neck. When she was through I looked in the mirror. If a fairy godmother had waved her magic wand she couldn't have added a more perfect touch.

The doorbell rang, and I jumped a foot. My goodness, I thought, what's the big deal? It's Mitch. He's been ringing my door-bell ever since he could reach it.

But when I went downstairs I saw he was no more Mitch tonight than I was Denise. In his winter-white tux, with a small cluster of mistletoe in the lapel, and his rust-brown hair shining as it never had before, he was Prince Charming.

He came forward slowly, and said in a voice meant only for my ears, "You're beautiful."

I blushed. Mitch had never said that to me before. "I love the corsage you sent."

"Kim told me you were wearing silver slippers, so when Mr. Petrini showed me some designs he could make I chose the silver bells."

I nodded and said, "You're wearing mistletoe. Did Mr. Petrini suggest that, too?"

He grinned, looking like himself for a minute. "That was my idea. It means you can kiss me if you get an overwhelming urge to."

"Maybe later," I said with an awkward smile. I couldn't tell if Mitch was joking or not.

At this point, Dad, who was driving us—as well as Kim and Randy—started for the door. "We'd better get going. The sweethearts of the ball can't be late."

We were almost out the door when Mom almost spoiled everything. "Your sweater,

Denny!" She hurried to the hall closet. "The white one will go fine with your outfit."

I nearly died on the spot. If she was stubborn about this I *would* die. "It's not raining," I said. "I don't need a sweater." I managed to speak calmly. Sweet reason simply had to prevail.

"But it's cold, dear. Neil, close that door while Denny gets on her sweater."

She was holding the horrible thing out to me—horrible tonight, with my divine ball gown, though at any other time it would have been perfectly okay.

For Mitch's sake I didn't want to create a scene. "No, Mother," I said in a very low tone that I hoped she'd recognize as the voice of desperation. "I definitely do not need a sweater."

"A scarf, then," she said, relenting a bit. "My wide woolen scarf. It'll keep out the cold, and the minute you get in the gym you can take it off. Be sure you check it, though."

She hadn't fussed so much about the pearls. "I'll be very careful with it," I said, figuring this was probably her best offer. I gave her a good-night kiss, then moved to the door, fooling around with the rather dingy white scarf as if I were about to wrap it around my shoulders, although by the time I got to the car I still hadn't.

"You can leave it in the backseat," Dad said quietly. "Just stow it away under one of the cushions so your mother won't see it later."

Bless you, Dad. He'd already backed out the car, and when he started the motor Kim and Randy ran over. They crowded into the front seat while Mitch and I got special treatment—the whole backseat to ourselves.

Daddy was going to let us off at the gym door where the other kids were streaming in, but Mitch and I were supposed to go in through a side door that led to the back-stage area, so Kim and Randy rode around there with us.

"What time do you want me to pick you up?" Dad asked. When I told him I'd call he said, "Just don't make it too late. You know how your mother is."

I knew how he was, too. *I'm with Mitch,* I thought, *so what's the problem?* But maybe tonight, with Mitch looking so handsome and mature, that didn't count the way it used to.

The dance committee took charge of Mitch and me while Kim and Randy went through to the gym. Last-minute instructions bombarded us from all sides. Smile, smile, smile, was mostly what they added up to.

While we stood there, waiting for our

musical cue, my hands began to sweat. I wished we could get started. No! I instantly took the thought back. I never wanted to go through that door into the gym. I wished I was home—a wallflower, only daydreaming about the dance. I was a fraud in every way you could think of. I wasn't Mitch's sweetheart, and I wasn't pretty. It was only an illusion. When I danced onto the floor I was likely to turn into Cinderella before the fairy godmother waved her wand. I could hear the cries of dismay as my lovely gown turned into ragged jeans, and Mr. Anthony's elegant hairdo collapsed into drab locks around my plain, ordinary face. . . .

Finally I knew I couldn't go through with it. I was dizzy. How could I dance when I couldn't even stand up? I clutched Mitch's arm for support—just as the orchestra struck up the first notes of our waltz. Somebody gave me a gentle push. Mitch smiled down at me.

"Here goes, Denny."

We went through the door. He started me up the stairs to the stage while he remained at the bottom. When I was in place, in front of the orchestra, the curtain went up. I heard a wave of applause, but it seemed so far away it had nothing to do with me. I smiled and twirled around once before moving to the side of the stage, the spotlight following me. I started down the stairs.

Then I felt Mitch's big, warm hand around mine. He led me to the place where the basketball hoop usually stood. . . .

I couldn't imagine the basketball hoop there now. I was vaguely aware that the gym had been transformed into a Christmas fantasyland, with twinkling lights, and green garlands, and crepe streamers everywhere.

In a minute I heard the notes that signaled us to dance out onto the floor. I went into Mitch's arms, and we waltzed down the middle of the room, while a wide path opened before us. We were cheered every step of the way. *Is this real?* I wondered, but when I looked up at Mitch he smiled, and his eyes told me that it was real, all right. *Just relax and enjoy our special evening.*

My heart whispered something back to him, but I wasn't sure what it was because the tempo of the music picked up then, rushing toward a crescendo. We whirled faster and faster, the length of the gym, then back to where we'd started. Finally, waving and smiling, we disappearaed back stage, deafening applause following us.

The committee received us with congratulations. We'd done a wonderful job, everyone said. Someone told us to take a moment to compose ourselves. "Then you can have fun for the rest of the evening."

When we went back to the gym we moved

onto the floor and were able to dance just like the other couples, except we drew a lot more attention, I guess. We were more dressed up than most of the kids, of course. Mitch was the only one wearing a tux, and I was the only girl in a real ball gown. The boys just wore good dark suits, and the girls wore dressy dresses. Kim was stunning in Christmas red.

My eyes kept roving and at last I saw Ty . . . with Marie. They weren't dancing but stood on the sidelines, holding cups of punch. Marie looked lovely in a green sheath that made the most of her height, and her vivid dark coloring, yet Ty didn't seem impressed. He was staring at me!

My heart jumped and missed a beat. Mitch glanced down at me in concern. "Did I step on your foot? Mom gave me a few dancing lessons, but she says I'm just like my dad, with two left feet."

"You didn't step on my foot," I said, "and with these heels you'd better hope I don't step on yours." I laughed, not wanting to tell him that I was so excited about the way Ty was looking at me that I'd almost stumbled.

When the number ended Mitch suggested we get some punch. My mouth was so dry I said I could hardly wait. But before we got to the refreshment table Ty barred the way.

"Hi, Mitch," he said. Then he turned his deep dark eyes on me. "May I have the next dance?" There was a husky note in his voice I'd never heard before.

Mitch put a firm hand on my arm. "Denise and I are going to get some punch."

Ty didn't look at him. He was still gazing at me. "I'll see that she gets a cup of punch, or anything else she wants."

I could hear my heart beating above all the talk and laughter around us . . . or maybe I just felt it. But was it right to go off with Ty when Mitch and I had agreed to take a break together? I looked up at Mitch. His features were impassive. Why wasn't he as thrilled as I was that our scheme seemed to be working? I hesitated a moment, then I smiled at him.

"I'll see you later," I said. "If it's all right with you."

He shrugged and waved me off. "Have fun."

Of course it was all right with him, I reassured myself. This was what it had been about all the time. Of course he wanted me to go out with Ty, or he wouldn't have agreed to the scheme in the first place.

I followed Ty to the refreshment area. Leading me safely out of the crush of people, he pushed his way to the front, then smiling triumphantly, he returned, holding aloft two cups of pink punch.

I thanked him when he handed one to me, but he said, "My pleasure—and privilege." He touched his plastic cup to mine.

"*Privilege*?"

My mind seemed to be wandering. I couldn't concentrate enough to figure out what he meant. Across the room Mitch was talking to a tall, plain girl named Joanne. Last year she'd sat on the bench all evening just like I had, watching the dancers. Her face, as she looked up at Mitch, was lit up like the Christmas tree that stood in a corner of the gym.

"Of course it's a privilege to serve the sweetheart of the ball," Ty said. He was giving me another of his deep dark looks. "It's funny, but I never noticed before how pretty you are," he remarked in a musing tone.

For some reason I remembered Mitch looking at me once when we'd been working on his bike. "You've got a smudge of grease on your nose," he'd said, "but don't bother to wipe it away. On you it looks cute."

"How's your wrist?" I suddenly asked Ty. For the first time I wondered if he'd really hurt it during the game.

"I still get a twinge now and then," he said, putting a slightly pained expression on his face.

The music started. Ty handed our cups to a boy who was passing by. "Put these down somewhere, will you?" he said. He'd led me onto the floor before the boy could do anything but look surprised.

I glanced around and saw Mitch again. He was dancing with Joanne. It looked as if she didn't know how to dance, but he was smiling and keeping up a lively conversation so she wouldn't worry about how awkward she was.

It was a rock number. Still, Ty put his arm around me and danced up close. "Listen, we're going to have that Coke at The Straw real soon," he said. "Just you and me. I'll get us a booth if I have to bribe somebody."

There'd be no better way to prove I was his girl. I tried to feel excited, but somehow I couldn't. "I'm not sure I'll be free," I said. He said something more, his tone urgent, but I wasn't listening. I was watching Mitch and Joanne. . . .

She looked almost pretty now as she gazed at Mitch with adoring eyes. She hung onto his every word, and laughed at something he said. Then a minute later his face bent to hers, and they seemed to be talking very seriously about something.

"Why don't we go outside for a minute and get some air?" Ty asked as the music ended.

"Not right now," I said abruptly. "Please excuse me."

I pushed my way through the crowded gym. I was flushed and confused and needed a chance to think. Why wasn't thrilled out of my mind that Ty at last wanted a dance with me? Why did I keep my eyes glued on Mitch? Didn't I see enough of him every day of my life?

I was the only girl in the rest room when I got there. I wished I could splash some cool water on my burning cheeks, but I didn't dare ruin my makeup, and maybe spot my dress. Back there in the gym I was still the center of attention. I washed my hands, keeping them under the water for a long time. I was about to go back to the dance when the door opened and Marie came in.

"Hi!" she said. "You look simply gorgeous tonight. I've been hoping I'd get a chance to tell you."

She didn't seem the least bit hurt that Ty had left her side to dance with me. Maybe she wasn't any more serious about him than he was about her. I was glad there were some girls that way. It kind of evened things up.

"There's something else I wanted to tell you," she went on. "We're being transferred again. We'll move right after the first of the year."

"Oh, Marie!" I cried. "I'm so sorry. You're just getting settled in here."

She gave a wry smile. "That's why I've never bothered to get settled in. This is the first time I've ever gone to a school dance. You know, I'll be really sad to leave Bayside."

"I'm sorry," I said again. "I should have minded my own business. I've just made things worse for you."

She shook her head. "I'm glad you told Carol about our talk, and that she wrote her article. I know now it's better to get acquainted if it's only for a little while than to brood about how lonely you are. You can bet that in my next school no one will find me crying in the locker room. I may even go out for the pep squad!"

I was so happy about my part in helping her that I gave her a friendly hug. Then I went back to the gym. The orchestra was playing again, and I went up to Mitch who was standing against the wall.

"Do you want to dance?" I said.

"You bet."

While we moved around to the music I said, "It was nice of you to dance with Joanne."

He smiled mysteriously. "It was nice of you to dance with Ty."

"What do you mean?" I asked. Did he already know what I'd just discovered myself?

"What do *you* mean?" he replied.

"Stop teasing me! You know what I'm talking about."

"Maybe I'd like to hear you put it into words."

"All right," I declared with a sudden burst of courage. "I'm not in love with Ty."

"Of course you're not."

"Don't tell me you've known all along!"

"No, not all along," he admitted.

"When did you find out?"

"I can't say for sure. I just slowly got the feeling you and Ty didn't belong together, and I knew that someday you'd wake up and see the light."

If we hadn't been all dressed up, and if everyone wasn't still looking at us as if we were celebrities, I would have punched him in the ribs for being so smug. . . .

A minute later I saw Carol dance by with a tall, familiar-looking boy. It took me a second to recognize him as John Lerner, editor of the *Bugle*. Carol had always made out that she couldn't stand him, so I was surprised to see how dreamy she looked, her eyes half-closed, and a soft little smile on her lips as her chin rested on his shoulder. Even in a simple flouncy skirt and a peasant blouse I'd seen her wear a half-dozen times before, she still looked different and dressed up.

"Look at that!" I told Mitch. "For a girl who has a nose for news, Carol can sure keep quiet about her own news. She hasn't said a word about dating John. I didn't think she even liked him."

Mitch looked at the dancing couple and smiled. "It seems to me there's a little liking there on both sides."

A buffet supper was served at eleven. I'd finally calmed down enough so I could eat, and I piled my paper plate with all kinds of food, making up for the supper I'd skipped. Mitch always ate like he was a bear about to go into hibernation, so we didn't say much as we sat in a corner and put away a few thousand calories.

I was doing quite a bit of thinking, though. Mitch and I would no longer be going together because of Ty, so what would happen after tonight? Would we go back to being just friends around school? Somehow that wouldn't seem right—not at once. We'd talk it over tomorrow, I decided.

When we went back on the floor Ty tried to claim me for a dance, but Mitch smilingly waved him off. "Sorry, Rogers, this dance is mine."

So were all my other dances . . . until the lights finally dimmed, signaling that the ball was over. I'd already called Dad and he was waiting for us outside. Kim got in the front seat again, but Randy, who lived in the opposite direction, had gotten a lift from somebody else. Mitch and I sat quietly in the back. In fact, we didn't really say anything to each other until we were left alone on the front step.

"Well, I guess it's over," Mitch said.

What was over? I thought, a sad feeling

coming over me. Did he mean the evening, or was he referring to the fact there was no more need for us to go together because I was no longer interested in impressing Ty?

Well, the evening certainly was over, but it seemed to me we'd still have to go together for a while, and I told Mitch so. "I don't see how we can let everybody down by suddenly going back to acting just like friends."

The porch light shone full on his face, and I could see he was frowning. "No, I guess not," he said. "How long to you think we should go on pretending to be—you know— sweethearts?"

I gave a tight little laugh. "After being chosen as Bayside's perfect couple I guess we have to drag it out for at least a while— maybe a week or two into the spring term."

He didn't say anything for a few seconds. He just stood there frowning. Then he said, "Yeah, I suppose that would be the thing to do."

Did he have to hate it so much? Had it been all that painful to pretend he was in love with me? I caught back a little cry as a sudden thought struck me. He'd been so friendly with Joanne tonight. Had he become interested in her without my noticing? She wasn't the type of girl most boys would be attracted to, but you couldn't judge Mitch by other boys—certainly not boys like Ty. Maybe Mitch saw something beautiful inside Joanne that nobody else saw.

"I guess I'd better go in," I said.

"Yeah." He shuffled his feet like he had the time he'd kissed me after the movie. Then his face came down to mine, more slowly this time—sort of deliberately, as if he felt that this particular night should end with a kiss. His lips brushed mine as lightly as a feather. Then he turned and ran down the path and through the gate.

When I'd turned out the lights I dragged myself up the stairs. All at once I was achingly tired. Mom stuck her head out her bedroom door.

"How was the dance, dear?"

"Just fine, Mom. I'll tell you all about it in the morning, okay?"

Quickly I closed my door behind me. Then I stood there in all my finery . . . that gradually turned to rags and ashes in my imagination. I knew at last I hadn't been a fraud that evening. Acting as if I were in love with Mitch had not been pretense at all. I'd been falling in love with him for a long time, only I'd discovered it too late. It was Joanne who'd looked at him with loving eyes, who'd been interested in his every word, who'd laughed at his jokes . . . who'd shared a serious moment with him, their faces only inches apart . . . while I'd used him only to attract Ty.

No wonder he could hardly wait to end the pretense that we were sweethearts. When I'd indicated I thought we should keep it up at least into the new term he'd frowned and said, as if the words were being dragged out of him, "Yeah, I suppose that would be the thing to do."

Even though I had only myself to blame, that hurt a lot, and I knew it would never stop hurting.

Chapter 12

We'd barely finished Sunday breakfast when Kim called, wanting me to come over.

"I'm asking Carol, too," she said. "She's sure been holding out on us. Did you see her with John Lerner, her big, bad boss, last night?"

"Still waters run deep," I quoted some forgotten source.

"Not so deep that we're not going to find out just what's at the bottom of them," Kim declared. Then she went on, "We won't be able to talk about this in front of her, so tell me now—how did it go with Ty? The way he started out I thought he was going to monopolize your entire evening, but then I didn't see you together anymore."

"I didn't give him a chance to monopolize

my evening," I said. "I found out I'm not really interested in him."

A gloating laugh came over the line. "I knew you'd wake up in time. It's Mitch, isn't it?"

"No, it isn't. We're back where we were before—just friends. We'll have to go on pretending for a while, though, or everyone at school will feel let down."

I heard a sigh of disappointment. She hadn't made much of a secret that she'd been pulling for Mitch all the time. "Hurry over," she said, and hung up.

Carol was already at Kim's when I got there. We all sat on the bed, and Kim grilled Carol like someone on L.A. Law cross-examining a witness.

"When did this big romance with John start?"

"There's no big romance," Carol insisted. Her glasses were pushed to the top of her head, and for the first time I noticed that her brown eyes were really soft and pretty. "We both wanted to go to the dance, so we decided to go together."

"Is that really all there is to it?" Kim leaned forward, eyes narrowed. This was the moment for a surprise witness to burst into the courtroom. But I decided to spare Carol.

"She told you why she and John went to the dance together," I said, "so why don't you knock off the cross-examination? Anyway, it's her own business if she and John just happened to go together or if they're engaged or even secretly married."

"That's not fair!" Kim protested. "I sure haven't kept any secrets from you. I told you both the very day I knew I really liked Randy, and here Carol surprises us with John. Well, now that we know about him, I want to hear details."

I found myself wondering if I could possibly be more grown up than Kim. My gosh, she'd been flirting with boys when I'd been playing baseball with them in the vacant lot. She'd been practicing with makeup when I'd been practicing stealing second base. Yet somehow I knew the time for the three of us to tell each other everything was over, and she didn't seem to realize that fact at all.

"Have you guys done your Christmas shopping?" I changed the subject.

Kim, whose allowance was whatever she happened to spend, pointed to a stack of beautifully wrapped gifts on the cedar chest against the wall. "Of course I still have a lot more to do," she said.

"I haven't had much time to shop," Carol answered, "but Mom and I are going to the mall after lunch. Then I'll wind it up in the next couple of days. With no school and no column to write, I'll have nothing but time."

"How's your shopping coming?" Kim asked me.

I mumbled something about getting to work on it right away. I didn't want to say I was flat broke even if I was. My outfit for the dance had run way over budget, what with all the extras, and I'd had to make up the difference out of my savings. I was too busy trying to think of some way I could earn a few dollars in the next couple of days to pay much attention to what Kim and Carol were saying—until Carol finally said she had to go.

"I guess I'd better go, too," I said.

When I got home Mom said Mitch had called, and I was to call him back. That had never been a big deal before, but now I could feel the pulses in my wrists as I dialed his number.

"Where were you?" he asked.

"At Kim's, for heaven's sake! Where do you think I was?" For some reason I felt huffy with him. But then he'd sounded pretty huffy, too. *Couldn't we even get along anymore?*

When he spoke again he sounded more like himself. "Do you want to look for cans tomorrow?" he asked. "The weather looks like it'll be good, and if we're lucky we'll find enough so we can turn them in."

"I could sure use the money," I said. This was the answer to my cash-flow problem.

Although we might not have as many cans as we usually turned in we'd get at least a few dollars, and luckily, Mitch said his dad would be happy to drive us to the salvage yard.

"What time do you want to go?" I said.

"How about nine?"

"Okay."

I thought he might say something more—like talk over the dance. *Or maybe something else.* But he didn't.

"See you," he said, and hung up.

The next morning I ran out to meet him. It was the first time I'd seen him since discovering my love, and for a minute I was afraid to look at him. What if he saw my secret in my eyes?

I needn't have worried. "What do you say we try Lookout Point?" he asked, all businesslike. "That's our best chance for some quick, easy pickings."

"Sure, let's try it," I said. While we biked up the grade I told him why I was so desperate for money. "My outfit for the dance left me broke, and I guess you've heard that Christmas is coming."

He slanted me a smile. "I've heard rumors to that effect." He paused so he could put all his energy into pedaling up the hill. "It was worth it, though—your outfit, I mean," he said, catching his breath. "I'll never forget how you looked coming down the stairs a your house that night—like a princess right out of a story book."

"And you were Prince Charming."

"Aw, shucks," he said.

We laughed, but we were a little bit awkward with each other. Something had ended for us last night, but we still weren't back to the easy way things had been between us before.

There'd been so much bad weather lately that not many people had parked at the Point since the last time we'd been there. I picked up the few cans that were out in the open, and Mitch beat the bushes without finding many more.

"Well, I guess that's it," he said after a while.

"Will we have enough to turn in?"

"Yeah, with those we have in the garage we'll be okay. Dad said he'll drive us to the salvage yard after work tomorrow."

That was good. It would give me a few days to go shopping once I got the money. Besides, I liked going to the yard. It was good to see the cans, and the stacks of paper and other stuff that were being recycled.

Mitch and I sat on the bank. I drank my cola while Mitch drank a small carton of orange juice. Coach Neff had gotten him interested in watching his diet. While we quenched our thirst we talked about Christmas. Mitch had a big family that would be coming from all over.

"And you and your folks will come over for Christmas Eve, won't you?" he asked.

"We always do." I added that Christmas night we'd have our usual open house.

It was nice to think about all the good times that were coming, but I had something else on my mind and finally I couldn't hold it back any longer.

"If you really don't want to go on pretending we're going together when school starts again it's all right, Mitch," I said. "We can say we had a fight over the holidays."

He tipped his head, studying my face. "Is that what you want?"

"No, why should I want it?" My huffy mood had come back without warning. "I'm through with Ty, but it wouldn't hurt me to go on pretending for a while that we're in love. I thought you might have a reason for wanting to be free, though."

From his scowl Mitch's bad mood had come back, too. "What are you saying, Dreyer? I don't like it when you beat around the bush like this. Usually you're pretty straightforward," he conceded.

"Well, thanks for that, anyway!" I snapped. I crushed my cola can and put it in the plastic bag along with the ones I'd collected. Then I swung aboard my bike, bu

Mitch stopped me before I could start down the hill. This was kind of like déjà vu.

"The last time you pulled this stunt you wanted me to pretend we were in love so you could attract Ty Rogers," he said, his green eyes blazing. "What is it this time? Are you picking a fight because you don't want to be friends with me anymore?"

"*I'm* not picking a fight—you are!" I declared. "And it's probably because you're mad that I want to go on pretending we're still sweethearts awhile longer. If you're so crazy about Joanne why don't you just say so?"

"*Joanne?*"

"Yes! You know—the girl you danced with Saturday night while I was dancing with Ty . . . the girl you held a lot closer than you needed to, and talked to, and smiled at like you'd been born for each other. *That's* the Joanne I'm talking about!"

For a minute he looked madder than ever, then suddenly he grinned. "You're cute when you're in a jealous rage," he said.

"I am not j——," I didn't finish the word because it struck me like a lightning bolt that that was exactly what I was. I grinned back at him, and he hauled me off my bike. I let the bike fall gently to the ground as Mitch put his arms around me. We were about to kiss when a car drove up and parked on the Point.

I smiled sheepishly at Mitch.

"Never mind," he said, smoothing a stray lock of hair behind my ear. "We'll have plenty of time together from now on."

Biking home, I couldn't wait to tell my folks that Mitch and I were in love. Then I realized it wouldn't be news to them at all. For the last two months they'd thought I was in love with him, and I'd never told them they were wrong.

Kim had guessed it, too, even though I'd told her it was Ty I cared for. I had a hunch Mitch had known the truth for a long time, too—he just thought I didn't know it, but luckily he was willing to wait.

I wondered if I was the only one who'd really been fooled.

Here's a sneak preview of *Right Boy, Wrong Girl*, book number five in the continuing FIRST KISS series from Bantam Books:

Like a perfect gentleman, Cooper opened my car door and walked me to Shanna's front door. "Did you enjoy yourself, Katie?" he asked.

"I had a great time," I told him. Watching *Gone With the Wind* last night had been fun, but going to the play with Cooper was even better. Shanna would really have a wonderful time with him when they started going out.

Cooper stepped closer to me and gently lifted a loose hair off my face. I guess it had slipped out of the braid. I expected him to tuck it behind my ear and tell me good-bye.

When he leaned down and his nose was only inches from mine, for a second I actually thought he was going to kiss me good night. But that was ridiculous.

"You're very special," he whispered just before his hand slipped around the back of my neck, and he gently pressed his lips against my mouth.

I don't know what possessed me, but I stretched on my tiptoes and kissed him back. There was a tingle inside me that reached all the way down to my toes. I was just about to wrap my arms around him when I realized I was cheating on Shanna. Guilt overwhelmed my body, putting an end to every last tingle of excitement. I took a deep breath and pushed him away.

"What's wrong?" He looked so cute with his hair mussed up on the sides that I had to turn my head away.

"I have to go," I said. Without offering any further explanation, I threw the door open and bolted inside.

Jimmy popped out from behind the living-room couch where the little fiend had apparently had his nose pressed up against the front window. He began singing joyfully, "Katie and Cooper sitting in a tree, K-I-S-S-I-N-G!"

"Shut up!" I yelled. I didn't care who heard me.

When he kept singing I covered my ears and raced upstairs. Crazy thoughts exploded in my brain. Why wasn't he in bed like any decent eleven-year-old? Shanna had been right about her brother being worse than mine.

I ran into the bathroom, pulled off my clothes, and jumped into the shower, hoping the pounding water would drive all thoughts of Cooper out of my head. Instead, the hot water reminded me of how warm and comfortable I had felt being close to Cooper. Shanna's Cooper!

I touched my lips and wondered how my first kiss could have come from my cousin's next boyfriend. It wasn't fair!

When I woke up Friday morning, my lips were burning. I could almost feel Cooper's lips against my mouth. My first kiss had come so unexpectedly, and I had enjoyed it just like I'd known I would . . . until I remembered Cooper should have been kissing Shanna! Trying to erase the memory, I buried my face in my pillow.

As my brain cleared, so many things started to make sense. I had thought Cooper was practicing his romantic skills when he complimented me at Zimmer's Ice Cream Parlor. But now it looked like he had been using my advice on me!

Although there was no one to stare at me and see my guilt, my face grew hot against the pillow when I remembered Cooper inviting me to lay my head on his shoulder during *Gone With the Wind*. By now, I felt bad enough about having tucked my cold feet under his leg. If I had rested my tired head on his shoulder, I would be too ashamed to ever face my cousin again.

Then I thought about last night and groaned. What if I had been his first choice for his extra play ticket? What if he had never intended to invite Shanna?

"Are you all right?" my cousin mumbled from her side of the bed.

"Great," I said into my pillow.

"You were moaning like you were sick. thought Cooper might have fed you greasy pizza last night or something equally disgusting." She sat up in bed. "If you're no dying, get up."

"I don't want to."

I hoped she would leave me alone, but she pulled the pillow out from beneath my head.

"I want to hear about your night with Cooper," she announced.

"I was home by eleven o'clock," I told her.

"And I was home by midnight, but you were asleep when I got home," she said.

Not really. I'd pretended to be sleeping when she tried talking to me. Last night I'd been too tired and confused to figure ou how to handle the kiss. Now I knew what to do. If I acted as though nothing unusua had happened, Shanna would never know betrayed her. Of course, I'd have to bribe Jimmy to keep quiet. I desperately hoped had enough money to buy his silence—otherwise Shanna and Cooper would never get together!